Heroes Don't
RUN

Other books about Adam Pelko by Harry Mazer:

A Boy at War

A Boy No More

Heroes Don't
RUN

Harry Mazer

SCHOLASTIC INC.

New York Toronto London Auckland Sydney
Mexico City New Delhi Hong Kong Buenos Aires

ISBN 0-439-79391-2

Copyright © 2005 by Harry Mazer. All rights reserved.
Published by Scholastic Inc., 557 Broadway, New York,
NY 10012, by arrangement with Simon & Schuster Books
for Young Readers, Simon & Schuster Children's
Publishing Division. SCHOLASTIC
and associated logos are
trademarks and/or registered
trademarks of Scholastic Inc.

12 11 10 9 8   7 8 9 10/0

Printed in the U.S.A.   40

First Scholastic printing, September 2005

Book design by Debra Sfetsios
The text for this book is set in Jansen Text.

FOR ALL WHO SERVED.
A WAR ONLY SEEMS TO END.
FOR THOSE WHO SURVIVE,
IT NEVER ENDS.

"Every man who's here, on this line, in these hell holes, is a hero in my book."

—Sgt. Bernard "Rosie" Rosenthal, USMC

Heroes Don't
RUN

Part One

Boot Camp

1944

1

In the summer of 1944, just before my senior year of high school, I took the train across country from Bakersfield, California, where we were living, to visit my grandfather in upstate New York. I hadn't seen him since before my father died at Pearl Harbor, and I told my mother that if things worked out I might stay and finish school there. My mother liked the idea. She thought I needed a man's influence.

What I didn't tell her was that I intended to join the marines as soon as I got to my grandfather's farm. He was an old soldier from World War I. He'd been wounded and lost his arm serving in the Austro-Hungarian army. His son—my father—had served too. He was a U.S. naval officer and died for our country. My grandfather would understand that I had to join up now, that I couldn't wait until next year when I was eighteen and didn't need anyone's permission. The war might be over by then.

"Good if it's over," my mother said. "Good. There's been enough sacrifice in this family. And if you have to go, you can wait until they call you, until your turn comes and you're drafted. Wait like everyone else, Adam. The war isn't going away that fast, anyway. We can only wish!"

But the war *was* going to end; that was the point. It had been going on for four years now, and people were saying it was only a matter of time before it was over. I'd break out in a sweat just thinking about it. I didn't want to be left behind. I wanted to serve, to be part of this thing my father had given his life for. I didn't want the war to end, and all I'd be able to say was, *No I didn't serve, I was right here the whole war, safe in Bakersfield.*

Living in Bakersfield, you'd never even know there was a war on. Yes, there was gas rationing and food stamps and Mom working in a war factory, but it was such a sleepy, sunny, boring place. One boring day was like the next. Hot summer days, and nights full of the sounds of insects. Bakersfield was killing me.

All I could think about was joining up. I'd wake up at night and feel my father right there in my attic room, in his navy whites, looking down at me in bed, wondering what kind of son of his I was. Saying, *Up, up! Sign up. What are you waiting for, son?*

When I told my mother I was going to visit my grandfather, my little sister, Bea, said, "I want to go see Grandpa too."

"No," I said. I was too sharp with her. Mom wasn't about to let Bea leave home at the age of seven, but I was so afraid my plan would get screwed up that I blurted out, "Just me!"

Bea's face swelled, and she ran out of the room. "Hey, Bea, I'm sorry." I went after her and tried to pick her up.

"Don't!" She was getting too big for that, anyway. "You're a drip, Adam!"

"Come on. Come on, don't be that way. You want to go for a walk?"

"Maybe I do and maybe I don't," she said.

We walked over to the playground, where I had to push her on the swing for as long as she wanted.

That night, after supper, I wrote to my friend Davi Mori. I had to tell somebody, and Davi was the one. He and I had talked about joining up for years now, ever since Pearl Harbor. Davi was in Manzanar, the internment camp way out on the other side of the Sierra Mountains.

Davi's whole family was there. They'd been interned along with other Japanese Americans who lived on the West Coast. It was a dirty deal. They hadn't done anything. It was the war, and they looked like the enemy, even though most of them had been born in this country.

> *Dear Davi,*
>
> *No more talk. I'm ready. I'm going to do it. You said talk to my mom. I tried that, and she said what I told you she'd say, NO. No, she won't sign for me. I didn't get excited, I didn't start yelling. It was frustrating, but I was reasonable. You would have been proud of me. But my mom—she was twice as reasonable. She's got reasons you wouldn't even dream of.*
>
> *She's afraid I'm going to get hurt, that's what it comes down to. Well, so I'll get a Purple Heart. Wouldn't I like that!*

What's my mother afraid of? I'm not going to get killed. Look what happened to you and me and Martin at Pearl Harbor when we were in the rowboat, and the Japanese bombers came, and they blew us out of the water. What happened? We got scratched up—well, worse than that for Martin—but we came through that okay. We're all still here. By the way, have you heard from big old Martin Kahahawai?

Next time you hear from me, I'll be in the marines.

Your friend,

Adam

2

The minute I boarded the train to Chicago, I said to myself, *This is it*. No more kid stuff. No more hanging around the house. No more mom telling me what to do. The train was crowded, people were sitting in the aisles and on the arms of seats. It was hot, and the wind coming in through the open windows smelled of steam and coal smoke.

I went looking for a seat, maybe for someone to talk to, maybe a girl. I imagined the admiring way she'd look at me when I told her I was joining up. The train thumped and rocked. Telephone poles, houses, fields, and barns whipped by. Every tunnel sent soot and cinders into the cars. I found an empty seat facing mother and daughter. Both of them had red hair—the mother's faded, the girl's alive, like a flame. She was young, maybe eleven or twelve. She was leaning against the window, looking out, when I sat down. The mother was reading her magazine.

I took out the envelope that Mom had handed me this morning before we all went to the train station. A photo of Davi in an army uniform fell out. It got me right in the gut. He'd beat me to it. I never thought Davi would get in the service before me. The grin on his face seemed to say, *Gotcha!*

"Is that from your girlfriend?" The girl was peering at me.

"Yup." I showed her Davi's photo. "Isn't she cute?"

"Oh, you're funny. What's your name?"

"Jane!" her mother exclaimed, and apologized to me. "You have to excuse my daughter, she's so forward."

"So *what*?" Jane flung herself back. "You ever think maybe I know him?"

"Don't be fresh."

Jane sprang up. She was tall, with freckles and that amazing hair. "Mother, please shut up," she said, and walked away.

"Did you hear that?" her mother said to me. "You're young. Tell me what to do."

"I don't know. I'm sorry," I said, wishing I wasn't there. As soon as she picked up her magazine, I left.

The girl was in the vestibule at the end of the car. The minute she saw me, she said, "I suppose she sent you after me! Well, save your breath."

"It's none of my business," I said.

"Did you see the way she treats me, like I'm a baby. How old do you think I am? How old?" she demanded.

"Sixteen?" I teased.

"Oh, yes!" she said. "You're nice! My name's Jane. Oh, you know that, don't you? What's your name?"

"Adam."

"Where are you going, Adam?"

"New York. I'm joining the marines."

"Oh, good for you! Oh, that is so swell! If I was a boy, I'd join right up. I would, no matter what my mother said. Do you have a girlfriend, Adam? A sweetheart? Do you have a girlfriend who will write to you and keep your morale high?"

"Not exactly," I said, thinking of Nancy, who used to live down the road from us. She'd moved with her mother to Oakland last year. We'd kissed once. Maybe I'd write to her.

"I wish I had a cigarette," Jane said. "Do you smoke?"

"Sometimes." I patted my pockets like I had a pack. "Girls shouldn't smoke."

"Boys do, so why can't I?" She looked around. "Uh-oh!" Her mother was making her way toward us down the aisle. "Here she comes. Don't you have just one ciggy, Adam? I would smoke it right in front of her, just to show her!"

"Jane," her mother said. "There you are. Come on, honey. Let's go back to our seats."

Jane yawned. "Oh, okay," she said, as if granting a huge favor. "See you later, Adam."

"'Bye," I said, taking out Davi's letter and unfolding it.

> *Dear Adam,*
>
> *My mom forwarded your letter to me. Good plan!*
>
> *Well, there's been a big change in my life too. Before, the government didn't want us in the service. They wouldn't even let us volunteer. Now every male in Manzanar, seventeen and up, has to register and answer a bunch of*

insulting questions. One was, would I fight for the United States. What kind of question is that? Maybe I look Japanese, but I don't think Japanese and I don't act Japanese. I'm an American, and I have the right to defend my country, even if it does stupid things sometimes.

Anyway, I heard that if I joined up, there was a good chance they'd release my parents early and let them go back home to Hawaii. I was one of the first to sign up. I got called every name in the book. Stupid, traitor, bakatare. Remember Sam, my brother-in-law? You should have heard him. "You little skunk, joining after what they did to us, to your father." He wasn't wrong, but I don't think I'm wrong either. This place is killing my parents. If my joining up gets them home a day sooner, it's worth it.

So I'm in the army. Look at the picture, if you don't believe it. I'm in the MIS. Military Intelligence Service, to you. I'm in a Japanese language school at Camp Savage, Minnesota. I'm going to be reading all those captured Japanese maps and battle plans. The recruiting officer here says that if we do our job, we have a good chance of shortening this war! With you joining up and me in it already, this war's going to end fast.

So, good luck on your plan. Hey, wouldn't it be neat if we met up somewhere?

Your friend,

Another Japanese American serving his country,

Private Davi Mori

3

In Chicago there was a change in time zones and trains, and a long delay. I wandered through the station eating a hot dog and stopped to listen to a marine recruiter. He was sitting behind a card table with a bunch of boys hanging around him.

"Go home and eat your spinach, George," he said to a boy who looked about as old as that girl on the train.

A poster next to the table showed blue water and white beaches and palm trees and a rugged marine in dress blues. The recruiter could have been that marine. He had two rows of ribbons on his tunic for campaigns he'd been in, and slash marks on his sleeve for years of service.

"Timmy," he said to another boy, "you're still three inches short." He straightened a stack of brochures. "I'm telling all you boys, come back when you have some hair on your chest."

Then he noticed me. "Okay, make some room," he said to the boys. He beckoned me over. "I want to talk to you, lad. You look like you're ready for the marines. How old are you?"

"Seventeen, sir."

"You're old enough and you're big enough. Here you are." He slapped the recruiting papers into my hand. "Take these home and have your father read and sign."

"It's my grandfather."

"That's okay. Your grandfather's signature, plus a notary, will do it."

"Thanks!" I tucked the papers into my pocket.

Once I was on board the Empire State Express, I looked over the papers. Nothing was too hard.

I slept for a while, but when I woke up, I started to worry. Why was I so sure my grandfather would sign for me? What if he said no? What if he said he couldn't go against my mother? By the time I got off the train in Syracuse and found the bus to Watertown, where my grandfather was going to meet me, I was convinced he was going to turn me down.

In Watertown I saw him through the bus window—still the old soldier, ramrod straight, his empty sleeve pinned back at the shoulder.

I grabbed my suitcase and ran to meet him. "Grandpa!" Seeing him, all my fears fell away. I dropped my suitcase, ready to hug him, but he held out his hand for me to shake. He crunched my hand in his, and I remembered the way he used to crack walnuts with two fingers.

"Look at this boy, Doris," he said to a woman standing near him. "It's my son again. Ja, it's Emory, God be thanked."

She smiled at me. She had a kind face. "That's what happens

to boys, Oskar, they grow up and look like their fathers."

"The girl that gets him is going to be one lucky girl."

"Don't embarrass him, Oskar."

"Embarrass, what are you talking about? We Pelkos don't get embarrassed." He insisted on taking my suitcase as we walked to the truck and rested his half arm, which used to give me the creeps, on my shoulder.

"It's great to see you, Grandpa," I said.

"The last time I see this boy, he was half this size," he said to Doris. "Now look at him. He's bigger than me."

At the truck Doris got in on the driver's side. When my grandfather objected, she said, "What are you worried about, Oskar? You know I'm a good driver. You talk to your grandson."

"Big boss," he grumbled, but he handed over the key.

That evening, after supper, Grandpa and I sat in the kitchen and talked. We had boiled potatoes and sausage, and there was an apple pie Doris had made. We demolished that, too.

"She's a good woman," Grandpa said. "Always there when I need help. Her and her boys. She's bossy, though. You have to watch her. But now that you're here," he added, "I won't be calling on her so much."

"Grandpa," I interrupted. Heat filled my head. "Grandpa, I want to say something. I want to—" I stopped and looked down at my feet. Big feet. I wanted to see marine boots on those feet.

"Well, go ahead," he said. "What is it? Say it."

"I want to join up."

"You want to join up," he repeated.

I nodded and looked at him, at his old face. "My father was—" I started over. "It's a tradition, Grandpa. Right? You first, then Dad, and now it's my turn. Now me."

"Now you," he said, and he looked down at his missing left arm.

We sat that way for a while, neither of us saying anything. Outside, the sun was going down. Shadows crept into the room.

"Will you sign for me?" I said finally, but maybe I didn't say it loud enough.

He leaned forward. "How old are you?" he asked.

"Seventeen."

"Seventeen," he said.

"Grandpa, I don't want to wait until I'm eighteen. I can't! I have to do this, Grandpa."

He shook his head.

I couldn't believe it. I'd come all this way, all the way across the country, all those hours and hours on the train, and now he was saying no. He was shaking his head at me. Just looking at me and shaking his head, letting me know in his quiet old man's way the same thing my mother had said. *No. No, I won't do it. No, I'm not going to sign for you. There's been enough sacrifice in our family.*

I didn't sleep much that night. I was in the same bedroom upstairs where I'd always slept when we visited my grandfather.

The moon was full and shone through the window, lighting up the corners of the room. Far away I heard a train whistle. Then a dog barking. Then, nothing.

The night was still and quiet, so quiet. Bakersfield had been quiet, but compared to this . . . I sat up and sank my head into my hands, thinking of the long months ahead until my birthday, when I could sign up for myself.

Around four thirty I got up and dressed and went downstairs. I moved around the kitchen, trying not to make noise. I didn't want to wake my grandfather. I found the bag of coffee, but no coffee pot. I boiled water in a pan and added the coffee and let it boil some more.

I was outside, sitting on the porch railing and sipping the coffee, which was really strong and tasted really bad, when the screen door slammed.

"A good time to be up," my grandfather said. He was wearing overalls and heavy work boots. He sat down in the faded green rocker, and it creaked and squeaked.

"'Morning, Grandpa," I said.

"'Morning."

"You sleep okay?" I asked.

"No, I didn't."

"Me either."

"Uh-huh." He nodded. "Thinking, were you?"

"Yes. Yes, I was." I looked down into the coffee cup and realized I'd drunk the whole foul-tasting mess.

"Same as me," he said. "Thinking. Thinking can keep you awake. I was thinking about your father, and you, and"—he motioned with his stump arm—"and this," he said. "This thing here. Maybe you won't believe it, Adam, but I'm not sorry. It was a terrible time, and it changed my life, but it's my life. Uh-huh." He rocked. "My life. And it is what it is."

I was leaning forward, listening to him. He was old, and he was wise. I waited for him to say more. Maybe he'd say something that would make me feel better about being stuck here for the next year, about doing things the stupid way I'd done them. But he just sat there rocking for a while, nodding, and not speaking. Until, finally, he said, "You got any more of that coffee?"

"It's not very good."

"Don't matter. You want to fetch me a cup?"

I went inside and poured the rest of the coffee into his mug, which he always left in the same place near the sink. "You want milk, Grandpa?" I called.

"Sugar," he said. "Two heaping spoons of sugar."

I brought the coffee out and handed it to him, then seated myself again on the railing. "What do we have to do here today, Grandpa?"

"Oh, same as always. There's always work to be done on a farm. But you"—he took a big swallow of coffee and patted his mouth with the back of his hand—"you got something to do. You got to go back to Syracuse and sign yourself up for the service."

"You'll sign, Grandpa?"

"Maybe not today. It's going to rain, and I got to rake the hay and start bringing it in."

"I'm going to work with you, Grandpa. We'll do everything."

"Good. And maybe in a few days, we'll drive down to Syracuse."

"And sign the papers?" I said again.

"That's what I said."

4

A week passed, and we still hadn't gone to Syracuse, and I was going nuts. I was reminding my grandfather every day that he'd promised to take me down to Syracuse, but every day there was something else that had to be done. I was afraid he was just putting me off.

The following week school started for the kids in the area. The school bus went right down Grandpa's road, and I should have been on it, but Grandpa didn't say anything. I wrote Mom a long letter about my trip across the country and about Grandpa and his friend, Doris. Not a word about joining up or school.

One rainy day we were in the house having breakfast after we finished morning chores. "Grandpa," I said. "Are you going to take me to Syracuse?"

"Oh, ja," he said.

"Let's go then," I said. "Let's go right now. I'll get the truck."

"The barn, there's a leak—"

"I know," I said. "I'll fix it. We can throw a piece of canvas down for now, okay?"

By the time we left, it was almost noon. Grandpa let me drive all the way down Route 11. He took over when we reached the city. He steadied the wheel with his stump arm and shifted gears with his right hand. It was something to see.

We did go to Syracuse, but Grandpa drove so slow, we almost got to the recruiting office too late. And then, when they sent us to have the papers notarized at the bank, it was closed.

"We'll come another day," my grandfather said.

"No, Grandpa! We're doing it today." I made him drive back to the marine office. "This is my grandfather," I said to the recruiter. "Why do we need a notary? You can see him sign the paper."

The recruiter looked at the paper, then he looked at my grandfather, and at me again. "Okay, lad," he said. "The marines want you."

I was ready to leave for boot camp that minute, but I had to take a physical, and that would be the following week. The next few days we worked on the roof. Grandpa was bringing shingles up and I nailed them down. During a break, he asked me if I'd told my mother I was joining.

"After the physical," I said, "when I'm really sure."

I went back to Syracuse by bus for my physical. I thought I might be a little underweight, but I passed everything. I was classified 1A.

A marine captain in a splendid uniform swore in a bunch of us. "In about two weeks," he said, "you new recruits will receive a letter telling you where and when to report. Have a bag packed, because you won't have a lot of time. Don't bring much money or anything valuable, just your toothbrush and a change of socks. The marines will provide you with everything else. Welcome aboard!" He saluted us, and we saluted back. On the bus back to the farm, I was so happy, I could hardly see straight.

Two weeks later to the day, the letter to report arrived. Grandpa and Doris saw me off at the bus stop on Route 11.

It was hard to say good-bye to my grandfather. "Grandpa, thank you." I wanted to say more, really thank him for signing for me. For understanding. For letting me go. For everything.

He rapped me on top of the head with his stump, the way he used to when I was a kid. "Use your noodle. Don't stick it up like a cuckoo bird and get it shot off."

"Yeah, Grandpa, I'll remember. I'm not going to get hurt."

On the bus I looked out the window till I couldn't see him anymore. Then I turned around and looked forward and thought about where I was going.

5

A bunch of us recruits were housed overnight at the Hotel Syracuse. The next morning we reported to the lobby at 7:00 AM—in marine time, 0700. We were counted and checked off, then lined up outside by the sergeant and counted again.

Then we marched down the middle of Washington Street to the railroad station on Erie Boulevard. "Close it up," the sergeant kept yelling. "Close it up."

We were all still in civvies—civilian clothes—carrying our suitcases and satchels, so people on the street couldn't really tell we were marines, but I thought they knew. I marched with my head up, my back straight, trying to keep time, but there was no cadence and we all kept banging into one another.

Once we were finally on the train, I dropped my suitcase on a seat, then navigated the aisle, saying hello to everyone. "Pelko," I said, shaking hands. And the other guys said, "Smith." "Weslowski." "Kaplan."

I offered my hand to the sergeant, but he ignored it. "When do we get our uniforms, sir?" I asked.

He glanced at me. "You got a seat? Sit down."

That cooled me off. I sat and looked out the window as the train picked up speed. Then I took out the Big Chief tablet I'd bought at the drugstore along with some other things and moistened the tip of my pencil.

October 10, 1944

Dear Mom,

Don't be mad at me, but I joined up. No, not the navy. The marines. Grandpa signed for me. Don't be mad at him. It's not his fault. I made him do it. I kept pestering him till he said yes. I passed the tests, Mom. They said I was in perfect shape, eyesight (20/20!) and everything. I'm on a train right now, with some great guys, on my way to boot camp in Parris Island, South Carolina. These guys on the train with me are from all over the East.

Mom, I know I told you I was going to stay with Grandpa, and I'm sorry I had to lie to you. But I couldn't wait till I was eighteen, like you wanted me to. Don't worry about school, Mom. Before I left Bakersfield, I had a talk with Mr. Leesum, the principal at my school, and I promised to come back after the war and finish up. I looked Mr. Leesum in the eye and gave him my word, Mom, so you know I'm going to do it.

As soon as we're through with boot camp, they say we're going to the Pacific, which is where I want to go. That's where Dad is. You know what I mean. This is for

Dad. That's why I had to join, Mom. That's why I couldn't wait. I'll write you and Bea pretty soon again, so you better write me back. Don't worry. I'll be okay. So don't be sad and don't be mad at me.

Your devoted son,
Adam

6

The train traveled east, picking up more recruits as we went. They got on in Albany and then in New York City—we got a whole bunch of recruits from all over New England.

I sat down in the dining car with two kids from Schenectady. Roy King was a really positive guy, and Andy DeMatteo seemed to enjoy disagreeing with everything he said. They were friends. "We signed up together," Roy said.

"What are you talking about?" Andy said. "You didn't sign up till I told you I was in. Where you from, Pelko?"

"Bakersfield, California."

"You should have joined there," Andy said. "There's a marine boot camp in San Diego. That's near Bakersfield, right? I was out there. My cousin lives in San Diego."

"I'm glad you signed up here," Roy said. He was inspecting the silver. "This is real silver, can you believe it?"

"Real silver?" Andy said. "You crazy?"

"Why not?" Roy said, "We're in the marines. Marines get the best. Am I right, Adam?"

"Is this seat taken?" a tall, bony kid said.

"Sit down," Roy said. "We've been holding it for you."

"Ben Bright," the new man said, but the way Roy and Andy went at each other, it didn't matter.

We all ended up sitting together, our seats turned so we were facing one another. We passed the hours talking, playing cards, and sleeping. We kept picking up more recruits.

At nine o'clock a Negro porter came through the car handing out pillows and blankets. We pulled the seats apart and lay them flat so each side of the car was like one long platform.

Roy had been saying all day that we were going to have Pullman berths. Andy gave him the needle about that. "Where's my deluxe Pullman berth, bacon boy?"

"This is perfect," Roy said, stretching out.

With our shoes off, and stretched out with our feet in each other's faces, the jokes started about who had the smelliest feet. Roy and Andy fell asleep, but Ben and I stayed up, talking. About this and that. About nothing, really.

"You hunt?" Ben asked me.

"I used to, with my father. Rabbit and pheasant."

"My father is morally opposed to killing animals. He didn't even want me to join the marines."

"He didn't stop you, though?"

"Couldn't. Me and guns." Ben half smiled. "That's my disease. Guns, hunting. The stalking is the part I like best. I once spent three days in the woods, stalking a deer."

"What did your mother say about you joining?"

He shrugged. "My mother's got nothing to do with it."

"I guess I could say the same thing." And I told him about getting my grandfather to sign for me.

Ben nodded. "Took the reins in your own hands. That's the way. We've got to make our own decisions."

I liked Ben. He reminded me a little of Davi.

It was late and I couldn't get comfortable. Lights kept flashing in my eyes, and there was a clanging at every crossing. As I finally sank into sleep, I told myself I was going to be the best marine there ever was.

7

Early on the morning of the third day, we reached Port Royal, South Carolina. We straggled off the train, hungry and shading our eyes from the sun. We sure were a bunch of tired guys.

A line of stake trucks was parked along the tracks, and a bunch of big, tough-looking marines was waiting for us. "All right, meatheads, shake it up," one of them yelled through a bullhorn. "Move! Get the lead out! Baggage in the baggage truck. Then get in those other trucks." He pointed. "Move! Come on, you dumb critters. We haven't got all day. What are you, a bunch of thumb-sucking babies?"

We scrambled up into the trucks. They packed us in like cattle. "Where are we going?" someone said.

"It's hot as hell," another guy said.

"That's where we're going."

Ben, Andy, and I were together. As the trucks jostled away from the station, I caught a glimpse of Roy's curly head in the truck ahead of us.

"Look at him," Andy said. "What are you doing over there, Roy?" he yelled. Roy looked around.

When we entered the sprawling marine camp on Parris Island, I was right at home. Parris Island was like all the naval bases I'd grown up around. It was all familiar—the gates, the guards, the even rows of low buildings. This was my father's world. My world now.

We unloaded in an open field and lined up. Names were called off. "Abbott . . . Andrews . . . Branch . . . Brennan . . ." A tough-looking two-stripe corporal quickly separated us into training platoons. I looked around for the other guys.

"Hey, turkey neck!" The corporal's hot, shiny face was up against mine. "I said eyes front."

"Sorry, sir."

"Shut your face," he screamed. "Did I give you permission to talk? Get out here, you." He yanked me out of line. "You stand at attention and don't move till I give you permission."

I stood there, my face burning. I wanted to turn, catch somebody's eye, maybe wink, because this was so unfair, but I didn't dare move. It was hot, and the sun was bright and in my eyes. I was afraid to even blink.

A buck sergeant, a three striper, sprang up on the back of a truck and addressed us. "My name is Sergeant Bessie. I'm your DI, your drill instructor."

He was neat and trim. He wore a garrison hat and starched shirt. He had creases down his pants, and a baton under his arm. He had that soft southern way of talking, but he was about as soft as a porcupine.

"You will address me as Sergeant Bessie. When you see

me, you salute, and you call me sir. The same goes for Corporal Peeler." He pointed his baton at the red-faced marine who'd screamed at me. "As far as you're concerned, I'm God, and Corporal Peeler is the apostle Peter. Listen carefully to every word we say, because if we catch you screwing up, I promise you, you'll wish you were never born."

As he spoke, I felt every word was directed at me. I was out there alone. I stood straight, eyes front. I wanted to prove to him that I wasn't a screwup.

"What you learn here is going to save your life," Sergeant Bessie said. "If you're fortunate enough to survive these next weeks of training, you'll kiss the ground I stand on."

While Sergeant Bessie was talking, Corporal Peeler strode back and forth in front of us, stopping frequently to thrust his head at someone and fix him with a fierce look.

Sergeant Bessie tapped his baton against his palm. "If I had my way, I'd ship you all back to whatever holes you crawled out of, but there's a war on, and I'm sworn to deliver battle-ready marines. I'm going to turn you useless lumps of dirt into marines or kill you trying. When I'm done with you, your own mothers won't know you."

He paused, looking us over. Finally he said, "Corporal Peeler, take charge."

"Back in line," Corporal Peeler ordered me. "Atten-shun!" he shouted. "Keep your eyes front and your mouths shut." He marched us one way across the field and then back. Back and forth. "Hup, two, three, hup, hup. Where'd you learn how to march," he bellowed.

It was a mess. Guys running into the man in front, guys taking long steps and short steps, and one guy who kept turning right when Corporal Peeler called left. Corporal Peeler pulled him out of line and handed him a rock. "What hand is that?" he yelled in his face. The guy was so nervous he gave the wrong answer. "You moron," Corporal Peeler screamed, "you don't even know your left from your right."

We marched and marched and marched some more. I thought it was never going to end, but at last he marched us to the mess hall.

The marines lined up outside greeted us with catcalls. "Here come the mama's boys. . . ." "Look at the hair. . . ." "Comb it while you've got it, Mac. . . ." "You'll be sorry." They kept it up, telling us how green we were and how bad things were going to be for us. Later I found out that some of them had arrived only days before us.

Corporal Peeler was almost our friend, pointing out where the head was where we could wash up, and then marching us into the mess hall and showing us where we would sit and where we had to line up for our food. "Take all you want," he said, "but what you put on your tray, you eat."

"Yes, sir!" we shouted.

The food was good. We had our pick of toast, pancakes, eggs, sausage, and home fries. I was so hungry, I took some of everything, even the white glop they called grits. I didn't like it. When we lined up to stack our trays, I saw that Roy had covered his grits with ketchup. "Some wise guy told me that was the way they ate it down here," he said.

One of the mess hall marines, a big guy, watching us emptying our trays, stopped Roy. "Eat that," he said, and made Roy lick up the grits, doggy style.

I scooped my grits fast and swallowed them before he saw my tray.

Quartermasters were next. We formed a line again and were issued supplies—two sheets, two blankets, two pairs of regulation dungarees, two shirts, and one dungaree jacket that they called a blouse. That was just the beginning. More stuff was piled on top of what we were already carrying: shorts, a web belt, a sea bag, a poncho and boots, measured by eye and tossed to us.

"Not boots. Boondockers, meatheads," the supply guy said. He had a pencil stuck behind his ear, like a store clerk. "Boots is what you are."

Trying to keep all that gear together, we marched to our barracks, a two-story wooden building. We had to climb the ladder (not stairs) to the second deck (not floor) and a long, narrow room, where we were each assigned a bunk and footlocker.

Corporal Peeler demonstrated how to make up a bed the marine way. "Now let's see what you can do," he said. "You've got five minutes."

I knew the drill, had learned it from my father on his regular Saturday inspections of my room. First tuck in and draw tight the bottom sheet, then the top sheet, then the blanket—everything pulled taut and tucked in the same way. I folded the second blanket at the foot of the bed.

I was the first one done, and I looked around to see if Ben or anyone needed help. Just then Corporal Peeler appeared from his room at the end of the barracks. "Atten-shun," I yelled, and snapped to at the foot of my bunk.

Corporal Peeler didn't find much that he liked. "Didn't your mama ever learn you nothing?" he said to one man, and then to another, "Tear it up and do it over."

He went right down the line, dropping a coin on each blanket to see if it bounced back. Out of the whole barracks, only a handful of us had it right. Two military school graduates and me. At my bed he bounced the coin, caught it, and said, "You! I know you. Where'd you learn that?"

"My father, sir."

"In the marines?"

"Sir. No, sir, navy."

"Navy! What are you doing here, bluejacket?" He made it sound like a curse. "You're in the wrong camp. This is the marines! You think you're better than the rest of us?"

"Sir?"

"I asked you a direct question, bluejacket. You think you're better than the rest of these boots?"

"No, sir."

"You think the navy is better than the marines?"

"No, sir!"

"What's your father know?"

I blinked, then I said, "Sir, he died at Pearl Harbor."

That seemed to really enrage Corporal Peeler. "You watch your step, cheeseface. I got my eye on you." He tore my bed apart. "I'll show you the marine way. The rest of you monkeys watch. This is the last time I do it. This is how a regulation marine bed is made."

Stupid, I thought. It was exactly the way I'd done it.

Easy. I could almost hear my father saying it. *Don't do that. When you're in the military, it's not like civilian life. You keep your counsel, you do what you're told. Even if you don't understand it, there's a reason.*

Afterward Ben gave me that half smile of his. "Corporal Peeler really likes you, Pelko, but he doesn't want the rest of us to get jealous."

That afternoon, after some serious marching that left me in a sweat, we went to the barbers. They were waiting for us, electric clippers and jokes ready. The floor around their chairs was thick with hair. "Don't worry if we take a little too much off. We've got some glue here, so you can paste it back on."

Sergeant Bessie picked out Roy to go first, because of his thick head of curly hair. "You, Shirley Temple, get up here, front and center."

It was over in less than a minute. Roy stood there with his hand on his naked head, looking down at his curls on the floor. He didn't look like himself anymore. Neither did I when they were done with me. None of us did. We were as alike as a bunch of naked chickens with ears, but when I put on the overseas cap with the marine emblem, I thought, *This is the way a marine looks.* Corporal Peeler, as he always did, put everything in perspective. "Maybe you think this makes you marines, but right now you're about as much use as elephant farts."

8

The next day, right after breakfast, we went for our medical. We were each given our medical chart with our thumb prints on it. Then we stripped down to our Skivvies and lined up. After that it was like a factory production line, moving from doctor to doctor to corpsman to doctor again. We were poked and prodded. It was, "Open wide. . . . Read the second line from the bottom. . . . Balance on one foot, now bend over. . . ."

When we got to the shots, the corpsmen had a great time joking. "Relax, Mac, I'm not going to break the needle off in your arm. Only happens once in a while." And then the corpsman next to him showed us a pair of horse pliers. "You guys are lucky. No more square needles."

"Funny guys," Roy said. His voice seemed a little squeaky. He was behind me, shifting from foot to foot. The next time I looked around, he was sitting on the floor, with his head between his legs, almost passed out.

That day ended with two dog tags on a chain with our names and serial numbers and religions inscribed on them. "Two," the private who threw me the tags explained. "One, the corpsman puts in your mouth when your luck runs out, and the other one he keeps for the record."

The next day started at 0500 with a whistle, lights, and Corporal Peeler ordering, "Off your butts and on your feet. You have fifteen minutes to fall out." We did calisthenics in the half dark, then cleaned the barracks, and after that we jogged, double time, to breakfast.

Back in the barracks Sergeant Bessie watched while Corporal Peeler showed us the marine way to stow our gear in the footlockers and explained the pails, soap, and brush each of us had been issued.

"That's soap for you dirt balls. You don't eat it. It's for washing your Skivvies and socks, and the rest of your gear. What'd you say?"

"Sir! Yes, sir," we yelled.

After a while Sergeant Bessie took over and started lecturing us. "I run a clean ship. No crumbs or cockroaches in my barracks. That means no food. Ever! And now, throw your wallets on the blankets and empty them out. You won't need money while you're here. Keep what you need for smokes," Sergeant Bessie was saying, "paper and stamps, that stuff. Store the rest of it with the chaplain or send it home. I don't want to encourage thieves in my barracks."

He walked up and down, checking our wallets, looking at the photos. "The same goes for dirty pictures." He stopped at Andy's bunk and made him tear up all his pinup photos. "Drop it on the floor. Now clean it up! The rest of you have any dirty stuff, get rid of it right now."

Later Andy told us, "It was just some pictures of Lana Turner in a bathing suit."

"Maybe she forgot to wash her face," Ben said.

For the rest of the day we were on the move, drilling, marching, doing calisthenics. It was snapping to attention, saluting, and yelling in unison, "Yes, sir! . . . No, sir! . . . Sir, I hear you, sir!" We stopped only for meals. That night, I was asleep the minute I hit the bed.

It went that way every day for the next six weeks.

Mornings we had fifteen minutes to shave, shower, and dress. If Sergeant Bessie found one speck on your face, he would have you scrape your skin bare with a razor for half an hour. There was punishment for everything.

If a guy was a little slow or didn't understand something right away, he was in trouble. He got pushed, prodded, yelled at. "Get the lead out!" We were all hit with that stick. We were all called dirt balls, girls, whiners. You could get yourself in trouble without even knowing what you'd done wrong and end up scrubbing the toilets with a toothbrush or "riding the range,"—being sent to the kitchen to clean the greasy grills with steel wool till you stunk so bad you couldn't stand yourself.

One morning I was mopping the barracks, taking wide sweeps, thinking I didn't join the marines to be a mop boy. I didn't see the DI, and my mop passed over his shiny black boots. I knew I was in trouble. I dropped the mop and snapped to attention. "Sir! Sorry, sir!"

Before the words were out of my mouth, he punched me

in the belly, sending me down to one knee, sucking for air. Nobody said anything. Nobody thought anything of it. It was what I deserved for being careless. I was lucky the punishment wasn't worse.

Boot camp shook the civilian out of all of us fast. Never enough sleep. Midnight calisthenics, and ten-mile hikes running with full packs, and Corporal Peeler barking at our heels, "You sissies, you friggin' goof-offs, you goldbricks!" Most nights, the lights went out and I was asleep, and then it was morning, and a whistle blew, and Corporal Peeler was charging through the barracks, dumping anyone still in his bunk onto the floor.

I did everything I could not to draw the DI's or Peeler's notice again. If we were running—and we were running all the time—I never let myself be in back like Roy. Ben and I kept telling Roy he had to try harder, stay in the pack, not draw their attention. I always tried to keep up with Ben, who was the best boot of us all.

Ben didn't look that strong, but he could run faster and go longer than anyone, so there was no explaining why Corporal Peeler got on him. But there was no explaining Corporal Peeler. He was like a dog with a bone. He just needed to have someone to chew on. It started with Ben's last name. "You think you're the brightest one around here?" Corporal Peeler said one morning when we were out on the drill field.

"No, sir."

"I say you are, Bright."

"Yes, sir."

"You're bright?"

"Sir?"

"Don't sir me. I say you are."

"Yes, sir."

"Bright is going to show the rest of you thumb suckers how push-ups should be done," Corporal Peeler said. "Step right up, Bright. Give me twenty."

Ben did twenty push-ups.

Corporal Peeler asked for twenty more.

Ben gave him twenty more.

Then he wanted forty.

Ben gave him forty. He was beating Corporal Peeler, and we all knew it. He went to one hundred and then to one hundred ten, and then he couldn't. He lay there, gasping for breath, with Corporal Peeler standing over him.

"Okay, Bright, on your feet."

Ben stood up. He never said a word about it afterward. It was the rest of us who cursed Corporal Peeler. We all hated him, and he hated us back.

9

Dear Mom,

Things are swell here. The food is great, I'm in a barracks, have a dry, clean bed. They keep everything superclean here. They take good care of us. It's hot, but it could be worse. They keep us busy, but you know what Dad always said, "Everything's got a reason." I know I have a lot to learn, and we have lectures and demonstrations. I've got The Rules and Regulations of the U.S. Navy down cold, and I've memorized the Eleven General Orders.

One of the first things I learned was that my weapon is a rifle, not a gun. Mom, any boot who says gun ends up holding the rifle at arm's length till his arm falls off! The marines are tough, but that's good for me. Don't expect to see the happy-go-lucky kid I was before I left Bakersfield. I see things differently now. I still have fun, but I'm not goofing off. I think about things now. I'm a lot more serious. Life is serious. Well, we're going to have to fall out in a few minutes, so I'll sign off.

Your loving son,
Adam, USMC

P.S. I hope you're getting the postcards I've been send-ing. I could sure use another letter from home, from you, and Bea too. It better not be a penny postcard, either!

Dear Nancy,

Remember me? I've never forgotten you. You were my best friend in high school, but I only heard from you once since you and your mom moved to Oakland. I thought you English-teacher types liked to write letters.

Me, why haven't I written? I'm not going to be an English teacher. Don't ask me what I'm going to be, though. Right now, I want to be the best marine I can.

My mother wrote me that she heard you joined the Women's Army Corps. You're a Wac, and you never told me? Well, I'm a marine. What do you think of that? I'm not the little green-pea guy you used to know. My DI here—that's drill instructor to you GIs—said he was going to make marines out of us or kill us trying. And he's sure trying! I've never been worked so hard in my life. Rain or shine, we're out there marching, drilling, doing jumping jacks, crawling through obstacle courses, and getting shot at! It's to teach us to keep our behinds down, so I'm not complaining. Except about the no-see-ums. I hate them. I don't know what you call them, but some people call them sand flies or black flies, or names you don't want to hear. They're smaller than a pinhead, and they swarm around your face when you're standing at attention and can't move. They bite! Tiny, red-hot stabs. Thousands of them. Some guys are allergic and their necks swell up like balloons. Maybe go to sick bay to get some relief, but if you do, you get called a sissy goof-off goldbrick.

Anyway, Nancy, you probably know all about this stuff. Army training can't be that different from marines. Ours is tougher, of course, there's nothing tougher than the marines, but I'm proud of you being in the service, and I told all my friends here about it. They wanted to see your picture, so how about it? I'd love to see it too. The army is lucky to have you. Why didn't you join the marines' Women's Reserve? Then you and I could have won this war by ourselves.

Your old friend,
Pvt. Adam Pelko, USMC

Dear Davi,

It was sure great hearing from you. How's school going? I know, you can't tell me. I don't think I'll be here too much longer, and then we ship out. Scuttlebutt is we're going to the Pacific, and if you do too, maybe we'll meet up.

I don't know what army training is like for you, but I don't think there's anything to compare to marine boot camp. Sometimes I think they're out to kill us. They sure want to break us down from being civilians and make us mean and hard and wanting to kill.

Yesterday I wanted to kill the DI, who went after one of my buddies, Roy King, for no reason. Roy's a really good egg, *always got a smile on his face. I guess marines aren't supposed to smile. We were standing at attention and the DI dug his baton into Roy's back. I didn't see it, but I heard Roy react. Another thing marines aren't supposed to do.*

He could have been court-martialed right there. Sergeant Bessie said, "Say again, mister?" Roy kept saying, "Nothing, sir. I didn't say anything, sir." I don't know how many times he said it. I was afraid Sergeant Bessie was going to club Roy or kick him cockeyed. He was screaming at him. He pulled him out of line. "You questioning me, you piece of dirt? I'll do any damned thing I want, and you keep your trap shut."

These drill sergeants are maniacs. They can do anything they want. My father taught me that about the military a long time ago. Sergeant Bessie dismissed the rest of us and left Roy standing out there in the sun for the rest of the day. No water. Nothing. He passed out. The corporal went out there and poured water on him, and then he made him stand at attention again till chow time.

I can't prove it, but I think they do it to get us so mad we want to kill. Them! Then they know we're ready to fight.

Write when you have a chance.
Your friend,
Pvt. Adam Pelko, USMC

10

In the beginning of December we were issued rifles: World War I, .30 caliber 1903 Springfields. "This is my first gun," Roy said. "Only gun I ever had before this was a BB gun."

"Rifle," Andy reminded him. "Not 'gun,' rifle." He had his rifle on his shoulder. "Finally, we're making some progress."

Roy was swinging the rifle left and right.

"You're holding that rifle like a canoe paddle," Andy said. "Look at me, on my shoulder, the way I'm holding it. Right, Pelko?"

"My dad always talked about the Springfields," I said. "They never fail, that's what he said. I was given one of these at Pearl Harbor." I had told them how I'd been a "marine" for a day, when I was just fourteen.

Ben, who had been standing there sighting his rifle, said, "You're going to love it, Roy. You want to hold it this way, Roy, firmly, against your shoulder."

We learned to field strip the rifles and reassemble them blindfolded. Drop your rifle, and you had to take it to bed with you for a week. A dirty rifle? Don't even think of it.

Toward the end of that month, we moved to the rifle range, a windswept open area off the ocean, bigger than a football field, with targets that were set up at 50, 100, 200, and 500 yards. We all wanted to get to that firing range, but I guess it wasn't our turn yet. Instead, what we got was mess hall duty. KP, kitchen police. Peel vegetables, scrub pots, and mop floors.

"First the kitchen range," Ben said, "then the firing range. That's the way we do it in the marines."

But there were more days—dry runs "snapping in"—practicing firing our unloaded rifles from different positions. Standing, sitting, kneeling, and lying prone. "Aim, breathe, and squeeze," over and over. We learned to zero in our rifles, adjust the sights, make windage adjustments, and change the elevation for long distances.

It was New Year's before we started shooting at the targets. The rules were strict on the shooting line. Point your rifle the wrong way, and you'd get slugged. Anybody could hit you, because you were a threat to everyone.

In front of each target was a grass-covered mound called the butt, and behind each butt was a marine who raised a paddle to show the shooter how close he got to the bull's-eye. My first day shooting, I thought I was going to do really well.

I was in the prone position. I loaded, locked, and waited for the range officer. "Ready on the right," he cried. "Ready on the left. Ready on the firing line. Commence firing!" There was an uneven crackle of gunfire. I wasn't ready for my rifle's recoil and it threw my aim off. I ended up with

"Maggie's drawers," the dreaded red paddle for missing the target completely.

To get out of boot camp, we had to score at least "marksman" on the day we fired for record. Roy was really worried, and we kept telling him, "You're going to do fine." He scraped through and got his marksman rating. Andy did the same. I got "sharpshooter."

Ben was the only man in our platoon who made "expert." The range instructor and all the other instructors came to watch him. No matter how far the target, he hit more bull's-eyes than anyone. Later I saw Sergeant Bessie talking to him.

"Bessie wants me to stay and be an instructor," Ben said on the chow line that night.

Andy gave him a thumbs-up. "Ben wouldn't do that," Roy said. "Would you, Ben?"

"Why? He'd be a jerk not to," Andy said.

"Then I'm a jerk," Ben said. "I'm not going to put a feather in Sergeant Bessie's cap."

When our orders were posted for advanced training, all four of us were assigned to the FMF, the Fleet Marine Force. These were the fighting marines we saw in the movies, the ones who stormed the beaches and fought the enemy hand to hand.

The day we left, Sergeant Bessie and Corporal Peeler came around to shake hands. A lot of guys milled around them. Ben walked away. I did too, but Sergeant Bessie came over to me and put his hand on my shoulder. "I expect you to make me proud, Pelko."

"Thank you, sir." And then I heard myself saying—and meaning—"I appreciate the toughness. I know it's going to help me be a better marine."

We shook hands on that.

As we boarded the train for Camp Lejeune, North Carolina, the new recruits were arriving. There was no mistaking them—the rumpled civvies, the same happy, dazed look that I must have had. "I feel sorry for those guys," Roy said.

"Not me," Andy said. "Nobody put chains on them."

I didn't feel sorry for them either. The truth was, if I felt anything, it was being a little superior. They looked young, green, and immature. They weren't marines, and we were.

Camp Lejeune was for advanced combat training. Everything we did there was with rifle in hand. We'd been issued new rifles, weapons of our own, .30 caliber semiautomatic MIs. They came sealed in Cosmoline, which was greasy, like Vaseline. We had to disassemble and clean every inch of them. After we reassembled them, we brought our MIs to the armorer for inspection and received our leather rifle straps.

We did calisthenics with the rifle, ran with the rifle, did bayonet drill with the rifle . . . parrying left . . . parrying right . . . screaming, "Lunge . . . thrust . . . *jab*." Different weapons were demonstrated. We learned about machine guns, the Browning automatic rifle—the BAR—and mortars and hand grenades. And we learned hand-to-hand combat with the KA-BAR, the marine fighting knife.

A colonel came one day and demonstrated a new kind of

hand-to-hand, judo. He asked for a volunteer and pointed at Roy, who always stuck out because he was so big.

The colonel was a tough little guy with a smashed nose and a chest full of ribbons. He turned his back to Roy. "At me, son. You're going to get me by surprise and slit my throat."

"Is that an order, sir?"

Everybody laughed. "That's an order," the colonel snapped. "If you don't kill me, I'm going to kill you, private."

Roy ran at the colonel, got his arm around his neck, and then he went up over the colonel's back and down on the ground. The colonel had Roy by the arm, with a foot on his chest. "I could break your arm now."

After that we trained twice as hard.

We left Camp Lejeune as the Twelfth Replacement Company. We had thought we were a tough bunch when we arrived, but we were a lot tougher when we left.

11

The train taking us to San Diego took two weeks to cross the country. As Ben said, "If Sergeant Bessie was here, we would have jogged and gotten there a week earlier." At the marine base in San Diego, we were given seventy-two-hour passes, a sure sign that we were shipping out. Andy and Roy took off to visit Andy's relatives in L.A., and I took Ben home with me.

At the station Ben got a hot dog with a smear of mustard. "Want a bite?" he asked. I shook my head. I didn't want to risk getting my uniform dirty. When my mother saw me, I wanted to look really sharp. I didn't even want to sit down on the train because I was afraid of creasing my pants.

"Sit down," Ben said. The train was moving.

"I'm nervous," I said. "I haven't seen my mother for seven months."

"Think she won't recognize you?"

"I'm afraid she's still mad at me."

Ben cracked his knuckles. "This is just between you and me," he said, "but my mother's in an institution. She's been a patient in a state hospital for twelve years. Sometimes she thinks I'm an attendant. Sometimes I'm her brother—or nothing."

"Gee, I'm sorry," I said. There'd always been something about Ben that was different. Now I knew why. Right then, I made up my mind I wasn't going to be blabbing about my mother all the time.

Ben shrugged. "It's okay. I'm used to it. Sometimes she recognizes me. Which is nice."

"You don't have to worry," I said. "I'm not going to say anything about this to the other guys."

Ben gave that half smile of his. "Especially not to Andy. He's a good egg, but he doesn't know how to keep his mouth shut."

I didn't have to worry about Mom or the way I looked. None of it mattered. She kept hugging me and kissing me. "God, you're gorgeous!"

"Mom, hey, Mom." I looked over at Ben, but he was grinning.

Bea was pulling on me. "I stayed home from school for you, Adam."

I kissed the top of her head. "Bea, this is my friend." Then she got silly and tried to pull my cap off. "Here," I said, and put it on her head.

Mom had food waiting for us. "Sit down, boys. Everything's ready." But the moment we sat down, she said, "Do you boys need to wash up?"

"Mom! How did I manage without you all these months?"

HARRY MAZER

50

Ben elbowed me. "Come on, lad. Your mother wants us to wash up."

I went to the sink, washed my hands, and showed them to my mother. "Do I get a gold star now?"

"Two," she said.

Ben finished washing his hands and hung up the towel. "I like your mother," he said. "Mrs. Pelko, I brought something for you and Bea."

He opened his zippered bag. He had a box of Fanny Farmer chocolates for Mom and a watercolor paint set for Bea. She went running off for paper and painted all the time we were eating.

Mom had prepared a feast—pork chops, mashed potatoes, creamed spinach, and candied carrots, and for dessert a chocolate cake with a whipped cream topping. "This is great, Mom," I said.

"Best chocolate cake I ever ate," Ben said.

"You've got a whipped cream mustache," Bea said, pointing.

Ben wiped his mouth. "Better?" he asked Bea.

After we ate, Ben said he'd clean up. He put an apron on, and Bea burst out laughing. "A man with an apron on!"

Mom wouldn't let Ben do anything. "You're our guest." He sat down with Bea, watching her try out the different paint colors on some old newspapers.

"Let's leave everything for now," Mom said. "I want to talk to you, Adam."

"What about?" I said, but I knew. This was what I'd been dreading.

We went into the bedroom. "Don't say anything," she said. "Just listen. I've been carrying this around for seven months. I'm glad you're home, don't misunderstand me, and I wasn't going to say anything, but I'm so mad at you!"

"Mom—" I started.

"No, please. Not a word. I just want you to understand, because of you, I'm mad at your grandfather. I know what you said to him, that old soldier routine."

"Mom—"

"You don't know how much you hurt me, Adam. You have no idea. Now you're shipping out and what if something happens to you? What am I going to do then?" She started crying. "I've lost your father already and—"

"Mom. Don't cry, please. I love you, Mom." I put my arms around her. "Nothing's going to happen to me. I promise you."

"Nobody can promise that. Don't you think your father promised?" She wiped her eyes and kissed me. "I want you to be so careful, when you're over there."

"I will, Mom." I loved her so much right then. "I'm coming back to you."

12

"Hey, you guys, where you been?" Andy said, when Ben and I got back to the base. "I've got some lovely ladies lined up for us tonight. My cousin set it up. The scuttlebutt is that this is going to be our last liberty."

Ben said he wasn't interested, and Roy had a girlfriend back home, so Andy and I caught the bus to San Diego. "What's my date look like?" I asked.

"She's a dish." He was combing his hair and whistling. "She's a friend of my cousin's, and if he says she's a dish, she's a dish."

"What if she doesn't like me?"

"Hey, you're a marine. She's a normal girl, she's going to like you! Stand tall, man."

We met the girls outside the Crystal Room. The place was full of sailors. We got a table and sat down. Andy's date, Veronica, was a really pretty girl who kept brushing her blond hair out of her eyes. I hadn't caught my date's name, and I didn't want to ask. She had big dark eyes, and when she looked at me, I didn't know what to say.

Andy and Veronica were talking, but this beautiful girl

and I hardly spoke. Every time she looked at me, I smiled.

This was the first time I'd ever been in a nightclub. Andy ordered Southern Comfort for him and Veronica.

"Ditto," I said.

"Helen?" Andy said.

"The same," she said.

Helen, I thought. Her name was Helen. "Helen of Troy, the most beautiful woman in Greece," I said.

"She was?" she said.

I nodded, hoping I had another sentence in me.

"How do you know that?"

"I guess I—I don't know. I read it somewhere."

She laughed, and after that she looked at me as if she liked me. Did she? I wanted to ask her. *Do you like me?*

Andy and Veronica got up to dance, and we did too. It was dark and the room was smoky. The band was playing "Begin the Beguine," and we danced close and slow. "Sorry I'm not a better dancer," I said.

"Oh, you're fine," she said.

"Helen."

"What?"

"Nothing. I just wanted to say your name." I was in a daze. I wanted to tell her she was sweet, sweet and beautiful, and I was going overseas, and I was in love with her. I wanted to ask her to be my girlfriend, to be mine, to write to me, to love me, to be the girl I'd come home to.

When we went back to the table, I asked, "Can I write to you?"

"Oh, that would be swell." She wrote her address on a napkin, and I put it in my wallet.

"Don't lose it," she said.

"I'm never going to lose it."

We held hands, and she told me she'd graduated high school and worked in a navy commissary. She was twenty. I didn't tell her I had just turned eighteen.

I tried to think of more things to say. If I said the wrong thing, she'd know how young I really was, and that would be the end. I took a drink of the Southern Comfort and lit a cigarette. "Do you smoke?"

She shook her head. "I never liked it. It tastes so bad!"

"Are you sure?" I offered her my cigarette, and she took a puff, then made a face, and we both laughed. It was great. Her lipstick was on the cigarette. I stubbed it out and put it in my pocket.

Part Two

Okinawa, Spring

1945

13

Dear Mom,

I'm just sitting here on the deck of the LST (landing ship for troops, to you civilians!) enjoying the view. All we have to do is keep our weapons clean and dry and exercise. How are you and Bea doing? Did you get over being mad at Grandpa? I sure hope so. Tell Bea that when I get home, we'll go together to visit him on the farm.

Well, Mom, I sure miss your cooking. Maybe you could send some of that chocolate cake we had. Ben and I still talk about it.

Tell Bea this morning I saw a school of dolphins, and I've seen flying fish, and the gulls are always around us looking for handouts, and one of the guys said he saw a whale. The best thing was a pure white albatross that stayed with us for a while. You should have seen it! Its wings were six feet, and it sort of hung in the air, hardly moving. Ben says that they make the longest migration of any bird, from almost the North Pole to the South Pole. Tell Bea she can take that to her teacher and wow her.

*And, Mom, the sailors say the albatross is good luck, so I
know you'll like hearing that.*

*Well, this is a pretty long letter. I better sign off
because I'm running out of space.*

Love from your son,
Adam

We'd been on the LST for over a week, and we still didn't
know where we were going. Everything was rumors, scuttlebutt that didn't mean anything. All we really knew was that
we were where we were, in the middle of the Pacific, part of
a long line of LSTs creeping along at a steady six to ten
knots. Once in a while we'd see a minesweeper. Mostly we
just chugged steadily westward.

We had too much time. Every day we disassembled our
weapons, wiped them dry, then oiled them, reassembled
them, and cursed the sailors whenever they sprayed water in
our direction. Salt and humidity were the deadly enemies of
our weapons. There wasn't much else to do except stay in
shape, stare at the water, and wonder what was coming—
and worry about enemy submarines. We'd already had one
scare. One of the sailors had spotted a submarine that
turned out to be a whale.

Then we ran into days of rough seas and the wind slap-
ping the ship around. It had made us all sick. Andy and I had
gotten over it fast, but not Roy and Ben. We were all out on
the deck. You couldn't go down below, it smelled so bad.
Andy and I were sitting opposite each other on a folding cot,

playing hearts. Ben was walking up and down with his hands over his stomach.

"Look at Roy," Andy said. "He's doing it again." Roy was hanging over the side of the LST, puking. "Hey, Roy," he yelled, "what do you want us to do with your cards?"

"Give it up," I said. "The poor guy's been at it for days."

"You know, it stinks here."

"Don't remind me." Even though the sailors hosed down the deck every day, you couldn't get away from the smell from all the seasick marines.

"Hey, Ben," I said, "do you want to play Roy's cards?" He just shook his head.

"Come on, Pelko, concentrate," Andy said. "I'm losing money here." We were playing for pennies. He picked up a card and threw it down. "So where do you think we're going today?"

"Same place we were going yesterday."

"Which is?"

"Guam. Philippines. Japan. Take your pick."

"Good-bye, Mama, I'm off to Yokohama," he sang.

Ben passed by and said, "They'll send us where they'll send us, and we'll get there when we get there."

> *Somewhere in the Pacific*
> *Dear Helen,*
> *Well, how are you? Have you been going to the commissary to work? What time do you go in? Do you take a bus? Or maybe your father drives you? What does he do?*

Well, I have a thousand questions for you, and I hope you have a thousand more for me.

Helen, I have to tell you something right off. I never thought it could happen to me so fast, the way I feel about you. I think we were meant for each other, but if you feel the same way, forget I said it. Let it be like we're just getting to know each other, and we're telling each other all about ourselves. So write back as soon as you can. I'll be looking for your letter.

Your friend (I hope your best friend!)

Pvt. Adam Pelko, 12th Replacement Draft, USMC

P.S. I never met a girl like you before!

14

Some days later, we started hearing the sound of distant guns, and that night there were flashes in the sky and then explosions. We were all up on the deck, watching. In the morning, we woke to find ourselves in the midst of an armada of Allied warships—more ships than I'd ever seen in my life. Huge, flat-topped carriers, gun-heavy battlewagons, schools of destroyers and cruisers, and hundreds of cargo vessels, ammo ships, fuel ships, and troop-carrying LSTs and tiny amtracs.

There'd been a battle here. I could smell it—fire and burning oil. I could see it—ships with holes torn out of them and clouds of inky smoke hanging over everything. The antiaircraft guns were pointed skyward, and the big battleship cannons were intermittently shelling some barely visible target. All we could see was a long green line that seemed to float above the water. It was Okinawa.

The CO, the commanding officer, assembled us all on the tank deck. "Okinawa is where you men are going." He was up on a tank. "The Japanese resistance is fierce. They know that once we take Okinawa, their country is next.

They're attacking our fleet with everything they've got . . . every plane they have, and half of them are kamikazes— suicide pilots crashing into our ships."

"It's Pearl Harbor again," I said to Ben.

"It's different, Pelko. We're attacking now."

I knew it was different. I knew we weren't being taken by surprise. I knew the *Arizona* was gone—it wasn't sinking here. And my father was gone—he wouldn't die here. I knew, I knew, I knew, but I had that same hollow tight feeling in my chest, half fear and half rage. *Now*, I thought. Now we pay back the Japanese for what they did to us, for starting the war, for killing my father. For a moment I thought of Davi Mori, then I pushed him out of my mind. Davi wasn't the enemy.

Our LST unloaded directly on the beach. The big cargo doors swung open, and we stepped off. No climbing down cargo nets with fifty-pound packs. No bobbing Higgins boats. No heart-stopping race for cover under a barrage of enemy fire.

No enemy fire.

The landing had been about as dangerous as stepping off a ferry. We didn't even get our feet wet.

We stood around on the beach like a bunch of gawking tourists and watched as the ship was unloaded. Ben, Roy, Andy, and I dragged our gear into the shade of an antitank vehicle. Trucks were coming and going, spitting up dust, and tanks clattered across farm fields. The beach was piled high with supplies, and our CO, Captain Weaver, put us to work loading up trucks. Boxes of ammo, mortars, explosives, coils of wire, communication equipment, and five-gallon cans of water. Ben and I stayed together, but we had lost sight of Andy and Roy. We loaded truck after truck. I sweated and swigged water from my canteen. By midmorning we were done.

Then our whole replacement company climbed up in back of the trucks, wherever there was a place. And we were off, down a dusty dirt road. It was good to be moving again. The breeze felt good. We passed neat farms, cultivated green and yellow fields, rice paddies, and little curving bridges. We saw Okinawans in the fields, and they waved to us. If there were battles going on, it wasn't here. We passed villages and the shrines where they kept the remains of their dead in curving stone structures.

It couldn't have been more than fifteen minutes, and we were on the other side of the island, looking out at the ocean again. We passed a cemetery sloping down to the edge of the water with what seemed to be thousands of crooked white crosses. It was our cemetery.

A veteran sitting near us crossed himself. He'd been wounded at Peleliu. His name was Dudley, a tall, easy guy, not that much older than Ben and me, but he talked to us like a big brother. "You'll do okay," he told us. Like most of the veterans, he didn't talk much.

We drove south along the edge of the water. In the distance there was a growing rumble like the sound of ten really busy bowling alleys. The sky was heavy. Clouds hung low over the ocean. There were fewer farm fields here and more hills, and more and more tanks and military equipment along the edges of the road and tucked between little knobs of hills.

As we bounced over one of our rough bridges, I looked down and saw a girl lying at the edge of the water. I saw her bare legs and her long black hair floating on the surface. I kept looking, waiting for her to move, wanting her to move. Soldiers died, not girls. I looked back, but we'd already gone past her.

15

The rain began when we reached battalion headquarters. Men, jeeps, trucks, tanks, and supplies were everywhere. Everyone was milling around. There didn't seem to be any order, and it didn't look like anyone was in charge.

We stayed close to Dudley. The three of us and a guy named Jake, who Dudley knew from before, found an abandoned half-standing canvas shelter and got it propped up. Jake went and scrounged up some sweet potatoes from someplace. We got a fire going and huddled under the canvas eating potatoes and canned rations. Except for the rain and the unending boom of guns, it was almost like we were on a camping trip.

That night I slept off and on through squalls of rain. Ben kept sliding into me, waking me up, and then I'd think of where we were, the thousands of miles of water we'd crossed, and this little island I'd never heard of before. I listened to the rain and the muffled rumble of guns and wondered what came next. I was just glad Ben was with me in all this.

In the morning we lined up for oatmeal and coffee ladled

out of garbage cans. I went off to fill my canteen, and when I came back, Ben was gone. Dudley said Captain Weaver had come by looking for a couple of riflemen. "He grabbed Jake, and then he got your pal."

I wanted to go looking for Ben. Maybe I could change places with Jake, so Ben and I could stay together. "Forget it," Dudley said. "You don't want to do that. You'll find your pal later. Or you won't."

I reported to headquarters after breakfast. "What's your name?" Captain Weaver said. He had a long, sad face, like a picture of Abraham Lincoln, but without a beard.

"Pelko, sir."

"I'm your CO."

"I know, sir."

The captain went through some papers. "Okay. Follow me, Pelko."

He brought me to where there was a bunch of unshaven, muddy marines sitting around, wrapped in their ponchos.

"Rosenthal," the captain said and nudged one of the marines. "Come alive, Rosie. Here's your new rifleman."

So that's what it was going to be, I thought. Just like Ben always said, the way things were was the way things were.

"What do you mean, *my* new man? I'm not in charge of anything." He had a bony nose and weary, red-rimmed eyes. He looked like a big parrot.

"The platoon is yours now, Rosie."

"No, no." He pulled his helmet down over his face.

"I'm not kidding, Rosie. There's nobody else." The captain didn't get mad, didn't pull rank. He was nice and even. "Steiglitz is out of it. You're my senior man now. If it's not you, what am I supposed to do, put this kid in charge?"

"Do I get a sergeant's stripes?"

"Guaranteed."

Rosenthal winked at me.

"Do whatever the sergeant tells you to do, Private," Captain Weaver said. "He knows everything." Then he left.

Sergeant Rosenthal looked me over and shook his head. "You're so clean," he said. "You have a watch on you?"

"Yes, sir."

"Don't sir me. I'm no sir. Just wake me up in forty minutes."

When Sergeant Rosenthal woke up, he went to talk to Captain Weaver. He came back with some more men, including Dudley, and we all loaded into the back of one of the trucks with some other veterans and green recruits like me. One of them, a big kid that everyone called Tex, couldn't stop talking. "Where we going? What's it going to be like? What do I have to do?"

"What you have to do is take it easy," Dudley said. "Save your breath."

I had all the same questions, but after that I kept my mouth shut.

"Does it always rain here?" a skinny kid named Joe Scanlon said. He was from around Boston somewhere. He had that accent.

"No, it never rains," Hartmann, one of the veterans, said. "You guys brought it."

The road was a muddy mess, and the truck slid from side to side, sometimes going deep in mud, then grinding forward. When a truck up ahead of us slewed sideways, we were all stuck. "Everybody out," Sergeant Rosenthal called. "Shake it! Let's move." He was in a hurry to get wherever we were going. And now we had to walk.

We were all loaded up with our rifles, cartridge belts, and extra ammo. I noticed that Hartmann had grenades hooked to his shirt, and I did the same thing. Another thing he and Dudley and the other vets had were two canteens each. Hartmann, who was a big guy, had the BAR, the Browning automatic rifle, over his shoulder. He gave Scanlon the tripod to carry.

"Loosen those chin straps," Sergeant Rosenthal told us, and pointed to the way his chin straps were flapping free. "You got that on tight, and a shell lands near you, the concussion will tear your head off. Now," he continued, still instructing us new men, "we move single file. No talking, and stay on the path. You don't know where the mines are."

We moved steadily along, mostly going uphill. All I could hear was the creak of our equipment and my own heavy breathing. The trail got steeper, and we were holding on to roots and stumps of things, when shots rang out. Dudley yanked me down. "Sniper," he said.

We were all crouched down. My heart was going a mile a minute. Everything happened really fast. I saw Rosie point to something, a thicket above us, and then he heaved a grenade and we were all firing.

Then it stopped, and Rosie said, "Stay down." I was gripping my rifle so hard my fingers ached. After a while Grasso went up to check. He disappeared.

We waited. There was a flurry of shots. Then Grasso reappeared, rifle held high. He came scrambling down the hill. "Let's go," Rosie barked.

We slogged on and came out at the edge of a huge muddy field. Everything was scorched and torn apart. The men we were replacing seemed to appear out of nowhere, coming out of the ground and moving past us, a long, weary, silent line.

The enemy was out there, somewhere. I wasn't afraid, but I was shaking. "Let's move it," Rosie said. He wanted us in the foxholes, two men to a hole, a green man with a veteran. "Pelko, you're with me." He gave the password and warned, "No talking, no lights. After dark, anything that moves, you shoot."

The hole we were in was a little forward of the others. "We'll take turns guarding," Rosie said to me. "You take the first watch."

Without thinking, I started to light a cigarette. I needed something.

"Put that out! They smell that, they'll come crawling this way like rats to cheese."

I pinched out the cigarette and put it back in the pack. "Sorry." I jammed my cold hands into my pockets.

"Don't say sorry. Sorry, you're dead. You gotta listen. You hear anything, wake me up. And don't fall asleep on me or we'll both have our throats cut." He wrapped himself in his poncho and was asleep in a moment.

I sat with my knees up, my rifle under the poncho, a grenade within reach. I was wet, but it didn't matter. I opened a K ration, but I couldn't eat.

Star shells were exploding in the sky, lighting up everything as they slowly descended on their little parachutes. Every time one of them burst, the field lit up and shadows moved through the bushes. I saw shapes. I saw movement, what looked like a dog, and then not ten feet from me, I saw a helmet rising from the ground.

"Rosie," I whispered.

He sat up and we listened. Rosie had his KA-BAR in one hand and a grenade in the other, but it was nothing. He said, "That's okay," and motioned me to lie down.

I couldn't sleep. It was a long, miserable night. The slightest noise sent my heart racing and every time a shell went over, my eyes shot open and I reached for my rifle. The shelling went on all night. Rosie had told me it was the ones that hissed that you had to worry about. But high or low, it didn't matter, every shell seemed to be coming straight for me. *You're going to get used to it*, I told myself. *You're going to do better. This is just the first day.*

16

The morning was gray and wet. We all squatted down behind an embankment, waiting for Rosie, who had gone to talk to the captain. Tanks and men streamed past us, crossing the field. The air rocked with explosions and the boom of mortars. "What would you guys like for breakfast?" Dudley said, breaking out the K rations. "We have cheese and crackers or . . . crackers and cheese. Tex?"

"You got something hot?" he said.

"How about a cup of hot spit," Dudley said.

Tex and Scanlon both laughed, but they looked gray, like they hadn't slept much either. Scanlon kept feeling for the straps on his helmet, and Tex kept licking his lips. When Dudley flipped a box of K rations to me, I just shook my head. I was too tight, too wound up, to even think of food.

Rosie came back, and we moved out along a narrow cut through some low hills. I was charged up, my heart pumping, more alert than I'd ever been in my life. My eyes were everywhere. We came out on one side of a broad open valley. On the other side were some steep hills that looked like loaves of bread. "They're in those hills," Dudley said, "like ants in an anthill."

I could hardly hear him. The air was exploding, bursting with noise and gunfire. We moved forward, crouched low, firing, darting from cover to cover. A tank was burning. Mortar shells came raining down. Shrapnel tore up everything it touched. It was almost like a battle scene in a movie, except for the bodies on the ground that didn't move. I ran, tripped, slammed into things. The air was smoke and fragments and men screaming.

A shell exploded and flipped me over, buried me in dirt. I couldn't see; I could hardly hear. I staggered to my feet. Where was Rosie? I began running and fell into a shell hole with Hartmann and Scanlon. Hartmann, his knee almost in my face, was shooting at a fortified Japanese bunker above us.

Rosie dove into the hole and told us that he and Dudley were going to work their way up around the side of the bunker. Hartmann got the BAR going. I raised up, pushed my rifle over the top, pushed in clip after clip. The barrel got so hot I thought it would melt. When I looked around, Scanlon's face was covered with blood. A piece of shrapnel had skinned him.

Hartmann had to tell me to stop shooting. Rosie and Dudley had knocked out the bunker with a couple of grenades. It was over. The rifle was trembling in my hands. I didn't know if a minute had passed or my whole life.

17

The next day it was the same thing. The Japanese were dug in everywhere, and we had to knock them out of each cave and tunnel. We started on the bottom of a hill, knocked them out of one hole, they barraged us with mortars and grenades, and we retreated, taking our dead with us. The next morning we went up again, and again we fell back, and we went up again.

We captured one hill, and there was another hill, and hills behind those hills, and more hills. And the officers urging us on, and us dashing from hole to hole, inching up like caterpillars or worms, till the lieutenant is dead, and the man next to me doesn't move, and the man next to him is screaming.

I saw Ben one day, but he was too far away for me to even reach him. I wanted to. I wanted to drop everything and join him. But I couldn't. I was here and he was there, and it would be like running out on my guys. And then he was gone, and all I could think was, *Okay, I didn't disgrace myself. I didn't let Rosie down; I didn't let the others down.*

We kept pushing. Men were hit all the time. Bullets

could kill you. Shrapnel could kill you. Sometimes just a shell concussion killed a man. I thought I was getting used to it, then Tex got it. He raised up for a better look, and a sniper got him right through the eye. Blood came rushing out of him. Hartmann bent over him and shook his head.

"Corpsman," I yelled, even though it was too late. "Corpsman!"

Every morning I woke up and wondered if I'd be alive by nightfall. Every night I was too exhausted to care. It helped not to think about it. After a while, you didn't have to tell yourself that. You didn't think about it.

One day Dudley, Rosie, and I were hunkered down together in a hole, and a grenade came rolling over the edge and landed between my legs. I picked it up and flipped it out like it was a nasty bug. The explosion showered us with dirt. Afterward Rosie patted me on the back, and Dudley lit a cigarette for me.

It never stopped raining. We were in mud all the time. We fought in the wet, slept in it, ate our soggy, cold rations in it. We lived with the shells and the mortars and the screams of the wounded.

One day I took a canteen from a dead marine. I didn't know him. He wasn't our company. I didn't look at him, just unhooked the canteen from his belt and hooked it on with mine. Rosie saw me. "That's okay," he said, "but I don't want you to get like Grasso."

Grasso was one of the souvenir hunters. After battles

they picked their way among the enemy dead, looking for stuff to send home. A lot of guys came up from the rear, enlisted men and officers. They ripped insignia from uniforms, pulled rings from fingers, even pried out gold teeth. Grasso had a sockful.

"If I'm here much longer, I'll start doing that," I said.

"No, you won't," Rosie said. "It's a brutal business, but I don't want you to be a brute."

Rosie saved me. He saved me from getting too hard. I loved the man. I looked up to him. I would have done anything for him.

18

After ten days we were pulled back to regimental head-quarters, where we'd spent the first night on Okinawa. We'd moved up to the front as part of a company of 250 men. Now there were only 50 of us still on our feet, not counting the ones with that blank, thousand-mile stare, who couldn't fight anymore.

Tex was among the dead. I didn't know anything yet about Ben or Roy or Andy. The first thing was to clean up. I hadn't changed my socks in two weeks. I had my first hot meal, drank cup after cup of burning hot coffee. Then I went looking for my mail.

I had letters waiting for me from Mom, Bea, Nancy, and Helen. We were all sitting around on the ground, reading our letters and passing around pictures. I saved Helen's letter for last. I read Mom's letter and wrote her right back.

> *Dear Mom,*
> *I'm sorry I haven't written sooner, but we've been real busy. Don't worry about me. Everything is going fine. I'm okay. Not a scratch. We got a little R&R, and I'm*

going to get a really good rest. I think about you and Bea all the time. I think about how much I love you both. I know that we're all fighting for our country, but it's for you, Mom. I can't tell you too much, but we're winning. So just don't worry about anything. I'll write you more later.

Your loving son always,

Adam

(Pfc. Adam Pelko, Company P, Second Battalion, 28th Marines, First Marine Division)

Bea sent me a cute letter. She had made pictographs all through it, so instead of writing *I*, she drew an eye, and for *see*, she drew a wavy line that was supposed to be water. Then, at the end, she wrote, "I love you lots, Adam, bzzz from your sister," and drew a bee for her signature.

It turned out there was no *letter* from Nancy, just a picture of herself in uniform. On the back she wrote, "Me! It doesn't show on the picture, but I'm a corporal now! We'll have plenty to talk about when we see each other again, which I sure hope we do soon." And then she signed it, "Cpl. Nancy Carver, U.S. Women's Army Corps."

I passed the picture around to the guys. Grasso studied the picture. "What's your girlfriend doing in the Wacs?"

"She's serving," Rosie said. He was lighting his pipe. "Like we're all serving."

"I wouldn't let my girlfriend go in the Wacs," Grasso said.

I took the picture back. "Number one, Grasso, nobody tells Nancy what to do. And number two, she's my friend and she's a girl, but I wouldn't say she's my girlfriend."

"Friend, girlfriend, I don't care what you call her, I wouldn't let her in the Wacs."

"Grasso," I said, "you're a chimp."

"And you, Pelko, are a chump."

I went off by myself to read Helen's letter. I was almost afraid to open it. What if she was writing to say, *Don't write me anymore*. What if she had a boyfriend? What if she'd just been acting nice because I was going overseas? Or maybe she'd found out that I'd lied about my age.

> *Dear Adam,*
>
> *Thank you for your wonderful letter. I've had you in my prayers every night. The first thing I did when I got your letter was look at a map. You're so far away! I was amazed to see that the Pacific Ocean is bigger than the whole United States, and you're out there! When I think of where you are and the danger you're in . . . it's hard for me to just write about ordinary things like myself. Next time expect a really long letter. I just didn't want to wait another second to answer you. Please be careful and stay safe!*
>
> *Yours,*
> *Helen*

It was a great letter. I read it five or six times, read it till I had it memorized. Then I folded it and put it in my wallet. I read it a couple more times again before I went to sleep that night. My head was spinning, and it took me a long time to fall asleep. Toward morning I had a wonderful dream about Helen. As soon as I got up, I wrote to her.

> *Dear Helen,*
> *I dreamed about you last night. I think about the time we had together. I go over every second of it, and I know it wasn't an accident that we met. Even if I never see you again, I want you to know that meeting you was the best thing that ever happened in my life.*
> *Truly and forever yours,*
> *Adam Pelko*
> *Company P, Second Battalion, 28th Marines*

I went to see if I could find out anything about Ben and Roy and Andy. Roy was there, sitting outside, like he'd been waiting for me. He'd lost weight, but he was still smiling. "Dear Jesus," I said, when I saw him. I was so glad to see him. We hugged each other. "Where's Andy?" I said. "You guys are supposed to be together."

"You know Andy. He always lands on his feet, except this time his feet got him out of everything." He said they'd been attached to Headquarters Company, carrying messages back and forth to the line. "We did a lot of running. But then Andy got a bad infection in his foot from all the wet, and he couldn't even walk. He wasn't good for anything. The doctors sent him back. He could be in

Hawaii now, for all I know, with all those beautiful girls, strumming a ukulele. The worst I got was this." He showed me where the tip of his ear was gone. "You think it'll get me a Purple Heart? What about you?"

"Me? I'm okay. I got dinged a few times, but nothing much. Just luck," I said.

"We're both lucky. So, where's Ben?"

"I thought maybe you would know."

"I saw him a few times with a tank company," Roy said.

At headquarters we asked about Ben. "Ben Bright," I said.

"He's our buddy," Roy said, leaning over me. "We've got to have a reunion."

The clerk, shuffling papers and running his finger down the lists, said, "Benjamin Brody?"

"No. Bright," I said. "Benjamin Bright."

More shuffling. "All right, all right, all right."

"Come on," Roy said. "That the best you can do? Shake it, man."

The clerk looked up. "What's he to you?"

"We told you, he's our buddy."

"He's gone."

"Gone?" I said, and for a moment I thought, Hey, lucky Ben! He'd been sent back too. "In Hawaii?" I said, turning to Roy and starting to grin.

"Hawaii!" the clerk said. "Sure, the one that's up in the sky."

"Ben Bright?" I said.

"Gone," he repeated. "Finished. Kaput. He's right here on the list from three days ago. Sorry, guys."

Roy and I walked out. Roy was cursing, and then he cried. "I can't take this. Ben. Ben! He was such a great guy."

I sat down on the ground. I couldn't move. I wanted to cry and I couldn't do that, either. I just sat there, thinking about Ben, thinking a million things. The first time we met on the train going to boot camp. How quiet he'd been. The way he'd always have some sly and funny remark to make. How he wouldn't stay with Bessie to be an instructor, even though it would have kept him out of combat. And then I was remembering what he told me on the train to Bakersfield about his mother. And how he'd brought Mom and Bea presents. *Ben . . . Ben . . . Why'd you have to do that? Why'd you have to get yourself killed?*

"You all right?"

I looked up. I'd forgotten Roy was there. I nodded. "Sure," I said, getting up. "I just have to be alone for a while."

We went back to the front with a bunch of replacements. You could spot them easy—they looked so fresh and neat, and they treated us with a lot of respect. I didn't feel like talking to anybody. If I had to say something, it was "Hey, Mac, give me a hand." Or if a guy got too nervous or started talking too much, I'd tell him, "Take it easy, pal. You'll be all right."

We went back to the same holes, the same hills, the same

stubborn resistance. We all knew the outcome—the Japanese were going to lose, but they fought us for every inch of ground. They were fierce. They were fanatical. They were dug in everywhere, in caves and tunnels.

We never went into the caves. We'd throw grenades, blow them up, seal them shut. But sometimes they'd pull a banzai and come charging out, half naked, with swords and spears. And we had to kill them. We had to kill every one of them.

There were too many bodies. So many shattered bodies. So many bodies without arms or legs.

I got through it. I did it. Days and nights blurred into each other, into one red fog. I did what I had to do. I moved when I had to move. I shot when I had to shoot. I was convinced that I was going to die. The sun must have shone sometimes, but I don't remember. I wasn't afraid. I wasn't anything. I thought I was becoming one of those men who couldn't fight anymore, the ones with the blank thousand-mile stares.

Rosie, Dudley, and I were in a shell hole so deep we could stand up in it. Rosie had Dudley and me throwing dirt up on the bank, and I must have stuck my head up too high, because Rosie grabbed me by the leg and pulled me down. "What are you trying to do, Pelko, get yourself killed?"

"He wants to die a hero," Dudley said.

"Hero!" I spat. "I'm no hero. I'm not brave. I'm scared all the time."

"Stop babbling," Rosie said. "You're a marine. You're here. That makes you a hero."

"No."

"Hey, I'm telling you something. Every man who's here, on this line, in these hell holes, is a hero in my book."

"Plus crazy," Dudley added.

"That's a given," Rosie said, giving me a grin. "Am I right, Adam?"

I shrugged. "Sure," I said.

"What are you going to do when this is all over?"

"I'm not thinking about it." What difference did it make?

"I'll tell you what you're going to do. You're going to school," he said. "Promise me."

"Okay."

"Say it like you mean it. Say you promise."

I was just starting to say *I promise*, when a mortar shell exploded on top of us. There was a moment, maybe less than a second, when I saw it coming and shouted, "Rosie!"

19

"Mac, Mac, how're you doing, Mac? Mac! Do you hear me?"

"Rosie. Where's Rosie?"

"Yeah, Mac, I hear you. Come on, open your eyes. Let me see those baby blues. I'm gonna give you a shot, make you feel better. Okay, soldier? You hear me?"

My arm was lifted. "How're you doing? Is that better?"

Hands on my chest.

"You okay? Let's see what these dog tags say. Pelko! How're you doing, Pelko? I'm Victor, and my buddy here is Gerstein. We're going to move you, pal. Okay? We'll try not to hurt you. Just hang on. We're taking you down."

The sky swung up and down. And the pain—up and down.

"Hang on, Pelko. Hang on, guy, you're doing great."

Part Three

Going Home, Summer

1945

20

Dudley lit a cigarette and held it for me. "How're you doing, Adam?" He raised my head up, so I could take a puff. "You know where you are?"

"Regimental—" My tongue was thick.

Dudley nodded. "Regimental Aid Station, right. You're going to be okay. You're going out to the hospital ship. Maybe Hawaii. Maybe the States. Maybe home! How'd you like that?"

"Good," I said. "You too?"

"No such luck. I got peppered a little bit, but I'm okay. I'm walking wounded. I'll be back up there in a week."

"Rosie?"

He shook his head. After a moment he said, "He landed on you, probably saved you. Saved us both. He took it all."

In Honolulu, at the Aiea Naval Hospital, the doctors said the blast had blown fragments of rock and dirt, all kinds of junk, into my body, even bits of bone. *Rosie's bones.*

They did a bunch of operations, cleaning out a lot of stuff, but not everything. They left some bits of metal that were too close to my heart to move. They did the best they could with my leg, which was all torn up. They were doping me up for pain, and I was doing a lot of sleeping. A lot of dreaming about Ben and Rosie. I was in and out of consciousness. Here, and then back there, with them.

I'd wake up muzzy and thirsty, and then I'd remember. *Rosie . . . Ben.* Sometimes I'd come awake shouting Rosie's name. Sometimes I woke up crying.

One afternoon a nice Red Cross lady came into the ward to write letters home for the guys. In the bed next to me was a marine named Bob Travis, who'd lost both legs. He still didn't know it. He dictated a letter to his father asking him if his car was ready, because he was coming home.

When the Red Cross lady was done with him, she came to my bed. "Adam? Would you like to dictate a letter?"

"My mom," I said. My voice came out funny. I was still getting doped for pain.

"What should I say?"

"Dear Mom." I stopped, imagining my mother holding a letter and looking at a stranger's handwriting. It would scare the life out of her. I shook my head. "Not today."

By the time I finally wrote my mother, I was sitting up, but my leg was still encased in plaster, lying there like a white dog that wouldn't leave my side.

> *Dear Mom,*
> *I'm in Aiea Naval Hospital. Remember? It's right by*
> *Pearl Harbor. Don't worry, I've just got a little wound in*

my right leg, but I'm okay. I'm going to be coming home real soon. They're taking great care of me. The doctors here are the best, so don't worry! That's an order. I'll write you and Bea again when I have some more news.

Your loving son,
Adam

A couple days after I wrote that letter, I got a bunch of mail from home that had bounced all over the place. I read Helen's letter first.

Dear Adam,

I got your beautiful letters. Thank you for all the things you said. Well, about myself—here goes: I live at home with my mother, my father, my grandmother, and two little brothers. Well, my brother Charlie isn't so little anymore, he just turned thirteen and thinks he knows everything now! My littlest brother, Billy, is only five, and so cute. We all love him to pieces. I think you know I work in a naval commissary. I love working here because I feel like I'm doing something for the war effort. But having that paycheck is great too! I give most of it to my mother, but it's still a great feeling. Once a week I go to a tap dance lesson—are you laughing? I started in junior high, and I just love it so much I hope I never have to give it up, even when I'm old and home with a bunch of little kids. My dream is to have six or maybe seven. Well, now you know all about me. Adam,

I hope you stay safe. The other day I was talking to a marine who'd been at Iwo Jima. He said if I had a friend in the marines anywhere in the Pacific, I should pray for him. And I am.

Helen

21

I thought when the cast came off, I'd just get up and go, good as new, but my leg looked like hell, and I was on crutches and weak as a baby. Even my good leg had about as much strength as a bowl of corn flakes.

"What do you expect," the lieutenant nurse said. "You've been lying around in bed. You're going to have to work to get those muscles in shape."

"Yes, ma'am." I gave her a really snappy salute.

"You've got to challenge yourself. That shouldn't be hard for a tough marine like you. I want to see you working hard."

"You remind me of my drill sergeant back in boot camp, sir."

"He probably told you the same thing. No whining. No slacking."

"Yes, plus a punch in the gut."

She laughed. "I don't do that part."

Putting my leg back in shape was hard. I went to the gym every day for physical therapy, but besides being weak, I was still pretty jumpy. Loud noises or sudden movements set my heart racing. Without even noticing I was doing it, wherever

I was, I scouted out places to take cover—in a corner, under a desk, along a wall.

Gradually I got stronger. I could really move on the crutches and spent more and more time out of my room. I ran errands for the men who couldn't get around. After a while I had the whole hospital figured out. My favorite place was the waiting room near the main entrance, where there were plants and places to sit, and I could watch people coming and going. I saluted the officers and smiled at the civilians, especially the girls in their summer dresses.

I was down there one day when a huge booming noise sent me diving for cover. I ended up on the floor with my crutches out of reach. A marine in a wheelchair scooped them up. "Here you go, pal. Those B-Seventeens make a hell of a racket."

"Yeah, I guess I thought I was back on Okinawa," I said. I lit a cigarette. "You smoke?"

"Do I breathe? Did you hear the news? It's over in Okinawa. They surrendered. It was on the radio. I heard it from President Truman, himself."

"Over," I said, leaning on the crutches.

I went over to a window, where I could look out toward Okinawa. Rosie. What a loss. What a big man. He loved us. He took care of us. When Tex's feet were so blistered he could barely walk, Rosie carried his rifle for him. He never seemed afraid. It wasn't as if he had a disregard for life—the opposite—he cared for life. But, he said, sometimes you had to do things you didn't want to do, but it was right to do them, so you did them. I didn't want to ever forget that.

22

I'd been meaning to call Martin Kahahawai ever since I'd come to Honolulu. I found his number in the phone book. His mother answered. "Mrs. Kahahawai," I said. "You probably don't remember me, but this is Adam Pelko. We met a long time ago. I'm an old friend of Martin's—"

"Oh, yes. You, I remember," she interrupted. "You with my Martin and Davi Mori in that rowboat when Pearl Harbor happened. I remember you came to the hospital to see Martin. How are you? You okay?"

"I'm okay now. I'm here in the naval hospital. How is Martin?"

"Martin? Good. He has a good job at the navy shipyards. I'm going tell him you called. Okay, Adam?"

Martin called me back later that day, and he said he'd come on Saturday, his day off. That morning I waited in the lobby for him. I was in my uniform, except I still had to wear a slipper on my right foot.

I was looking at the tropical fish tank when he tapped me on the shoulder. "Martin!" I'd forgotten what a big guy he was. I wanted to hug him, but the crutches got in the way.

"What happened to you?" he said. "Can you walk?"

"What does it look like?"

"Okay, come on then. I got one big surprise for you." Outside, he pointed across the parking lot. "There," he said. "That Chevy truck. It's in there. That as fast as you can go?"

"This is high gear," I said, hopping after him.

He looked back at me. "Still one big funny haole. Go look and see your surprise, Adam."

A soldier was sitting in front. It was Davi Mori.

When he saw me, he sprang out of the car, a grin all over his face, and started pounding me.

"What's with the crutches?"

"Where the heck did you come from, Mori?"

"You like my surprise?"

The three of us were all talking at once.

Davi was home on furlough visiting his family and friends.

We got in the truck. Davi was at the wheel, Martin in the middle, and I sat on the outside because of my leg. Martin put his arms around us.

"You two guys—you are my big heroes," he said.

"The two of us together aren't as big as you, Kahahawai," Davi said.

"How'd you stay out?" I said.

"I tried to enlist. I don't want you guys to think I'm a slacker. I tried the army, the navy. I even tried the marines. Nobody wanted me. Why?" He pointed to his ear. "I don't hear too good, compliments of the Japanese at Pearl Harbor.

Remember how low those bombers came? And those bombs, and the one that flipped us? They say that's what did it."

"The Japanese were lucky they didn't have to fight you," Davi said. "If you were in, K, the war would be over by now."

It was almost the way it used to be, the three of us, going at one another nonstop.

"Hey, Adam, you know what the Japanese said about you marines?" Davi started the truck. "They said you guys weren't human beings. They knew you were devils recruited from jails and lunatic asylums."

Martin laughed. "Good story."

"No, I mean it," Davi said. "I interrogated enough prisoners."

"They were the crazy ones," I said. "The way they never gave up."

In the heights over Pearl Harbor we got out of the truck and stood at the fence, the same place where we'd stood four years earlier. That morning we'd stashed our bikes, slipped under the fence, and slid down the hill to the shore. Three kids poking around, picking up rocks and looking for stuff. We'd found a rowboat.

"Remember?" Davi said. "That day, it was just like this, the same blue sky."

Martin was nodding and smiling. Of the three of us, I thought he was the least changed, the same big and enthusiastic guy he'd always been. But Davi was different, older— there was something thick in him now, solid, like a tree.

"Let's go down the hill, maybe find a boat," Martin said, "and go for a row."

"What, and start World War Three?" Davi said.

The two of them went down the hill, laughing and poking each other. I stayed by the fence, looking out over the water, to Ford Island, where my father's ship lay, where he lay. A breeze had sprung up. *I miss you, Dad.*

Part Four

Home,
Summer
1945

23

It was night when our ship reached the United States. Everybody who could walk was up on deck. In the distance I saw the dark mass of the continent, then the lights of San Francisco Harbor. Someone began singing "America the Beautiful." Another voice joined his and another and then we were all cheering and singing. Tears, too.

As soon as we docked, I called my mother. "Adam? Is it really you? Are you really all right?"

"Oh, Mom." My voice cracked. "I'll be home soon. I have to go to San Diego. I'll be getting leave and coming home."

"Oh, lord! It's so good to hear your voice! Wait a moment. Say hello to your sister."

Bea came on. "Adam, I'm taller. You're going to be surprised when you see me. I grew one whole inch. Good-bye."

My mother came on again. "Come home quickly. I can't wait to see you."

"Mom, I'll come as fast as I can."

After I hung up with my mother, I got the operator and gave her my grandfather's number in Watertown, New

York. I heard her say, "I have a long distance call for Oskar Pelko."

"Who is it?" I heard my grandfather's voice.

"Grandpa, it's me, Adam."

"Just a moment, sir. Is this Oskar Pelko?"

"What else?" my grandfather said. "Adam? Is it you? Where are you?"

"I'm home, Grandpa. In California. How are you doing?"

"Good enough. Never mind me. How are you? What happened?"

"I'm okay. I'm not dead yet, Grandpa."

"I can tell that, but I know something happened. I had this dream that you were in a fire."

"I took a little shrapnel, Grandpa, but I'm all right now."

"The dream was bad. Everything was burning. The whole house. You were trying to get out, but there was no way out. It was terrible. I couldn't sleep afterward."

"Grandpa, I wish I could see you right now."

"I thought about you every day." He started to cry. It made me cry too. "I want to see you with my own eyes."

"I'll come, Grandpa. I promise."

In San Diego, at the marine hospital, I was checked over. I was using a cane now. I only had to get my leave papers, and I'd be going home. Everyone in the hospital was talking about a new kind of bomb that we had just used in Japan. The significance of it didn't register, though, until a few days later, when I was getting ready to go on leave.

Bells were clanging all over the city. Japan had surrendered. The war was over. People went nuts—me too—hugging and kissing, and dancing in the streets.

I'd been putting off calling Helen. It was stupid to be scared, but I was. Her father answered the phone, and I almost hung up. *Grow up*, I said to myself. *You're a marine, you jerk.*

"Sir. My name is Adam Pelko. Will you tell Helen I called? I'm taking the seven fifty-eight morning train to Bakersfield, and I wanted to say hello before I left."

"I know about you," he said. "You're in the marines. Where are you stationed?"

"I'm at the marine hospital."

"You were wounded?"

"Yes, sir."

"I want to say thank you, Adam, for everything you men have done for our country."

"Thank you, sir."

"Helen's away tonight, but I'll let her know you called."

When I hung up, I stood there banging my head on the wall. *Away.* I'd waited too long, and there was nobody to blame but me.

The next morning I was standing on the platform, waiting to board the train, when I saw Helen running toward me. She flung her arms around me, and we had a long, sweet, unbelievable hug.

"I thought I was going to miss you," she said.

I couldn't stop staring at her. I'd forgotten how perfect she was.

We both started talking at once, but there was no time. The conductor was calling, "All aboard."

"Do you have to go?"

"I haven't seen my mother yet. Or my little sister. But I'll come back, if you want me to."

"I want you to."

I took her hand. I wanted to kiss her, I didn't want to leave, but the train was beginning to move.

24

The first few days I was home, I slept almost around the clock. I had thought I would do all sorts of things—see who was around that I knew, and at the very least go back to the high school and talk to Mr. Ewing, my old history teacher, and Mr. Leesum, the principal. But I was tired, and I didn't do anything but sleep and eat and talk to Mom.

I showed her Nancy's picture and told her a little bit about Helen. I didn't talk much about the war. She wanted to know about my wounds, and I told her a little, but I saw how hard it was for her to hear. Mostly we talked about normal stuff. Her work—she was an inspector now in the war plant—and she talked about Bea, how she'd really matured. "She comes home after school, she washes the dishes, she makes a salad—"

"Wait a second," I said. "Is that my little sister, Miss Ball of Fire, you're talking about?"

"You're not the only one who's changed, Adam. We've all gone through a lot."

"I know, Mom. I'm sorry."

She was quiet, and I was too. I thought of myself a year ago, how much I'd wanted it, wanted to go in, to fight, to be tough and invincible. I knew I might get hurt or even die, but they were just words. Which was strange, considering what I'd seen at Pearl Harbor. And yet, until Okinawa, I didn't really believe that I could die, or that Ben would, or Rosie.

And another thing I'd never realized—how hard it had been for Mom. Dad dying. And then me, her never knowing where I was or if I was even alive. I thought when they gave me the Purple Heart, I was going to give it to her. I was going to say, *It's for you too, Mom.*

Every day I'd go downtown. I needed to walk a lot to keep my leg from stiffening up. It looked to me like nothing had changed in Bakersfield. I liked that now. I drank up the ordinariness of it.

People stopped to talk to me. They'd shake my hand, call me hero, and tell me how proud they were of me. And then they'd ask me what it had been like, what it had "really" been like.

At first I'd stand there and talk. I told them things— things I'd seen, things that had really happened to me—and they'd say, "Awful . . . oh, my goodness . . . Is that so?" I talked and talked. I talked too much. I came home from those walks feeling like a phony, like all that talk had obliterated Rosie and Ben.

Civilians didn't understand. They thought that battle was about bravery and heroes and raising the flag on top of

Mount Surabachi. They didn't see the dead scattered over the hillsides, stacked in ditches, our men, their men. Dead on dead. How could I ever explain? There was just no connection between the battlefield and Bakersfield. Between that meat grinder and this peaceful little town.

"Just be glad you weren't there," I'd say. That's one thing I did say. And about being a hero, I said, "There were a lot of heroes. Most of them never got a medal or came home."

And later, when I got home, I'd be so tired I wouldn't even get up the stairs. I'd just hit the deck outside and be asleep in a minute.

One day I was down at the creek with Bea. We squatted at the water's edge. She caught a frog and handed it to me. "What do I do with this?" I said.

"Hold it," she said. "I have to catch her boyfriend."

I sat down on a rock. I had my boondockers off and my pants rolled up. The sun felt good on my leg, and I thought, *Here I am . . . here I am with my sister.* I cried a little, and I couldn't wipe my eyes because of the frog, which made me laugh. The willows at the side of the river shone in the sun. I sat there, holding Bea's frog, and feeling the wind, and watching the leaves dance in the light, and thinking how beautiful the world was, how it was full of wind and sunlight and frogs.

There was another world, a dark world of guns and death, but that world was over, maybe forever. We'd made a better world. It was the only way to understand why my father had died and Ben and Rosie and all the others. I watched Bea squatting at the edge of the water, the sun striking her hair, and I was so glad that she would never have to know anything about war.

The Battle for Okinawa—

An Historical Note

"You're an old-timer if you survive twenty-four hours."
—World War II combat soldier

Okinawa is some three hundred nautical miles from Japan, the largest of the Ryukyu chain of islands. From it, the Allies launched the final assault on the Japanese mainland. But as it happened, the battle for Okinawa was the last major battle of World War II.

The U.S. attack force approaching Okinawa consisted of 1,381 ships, and carried 746,000 tons of supplies and 183,000 troops. Altogether, nearly half a million men were involved in moving cargo to Okinawa from ports all around the Pacific Ocean.

The Japanese naval forces that might have opposed the Americans had been largely destroyed. Their only hope of slowing the approaching American armada was their kamikaze suicide planes. Kamikaze means "divine wind," a reference to a typhoon in the year 1281 that drove back Kublai Khan's armada and kept it from invading Japan, as the Americans were now. Kamikaze pilots were young volunteers, long on courage and short on experience, who were eager to give their lives for their country. They wore white headbands signifying death, and before their final suicide flights they attended their own funerals, sending farewell letters to their families along with little white boxes containing bits of their hair and nails, all that would remain of them after they crashed into the American ships. The Japanese war had become a suicide war.

Close to two thousand separate kamikaze attacks were launched during the Okinawa campaign. They sank or damaged 368 American ships, killing or wounding 9,700 sailors, the greatest one-battle loss in U.S. Naval history.

On April 1, 1945, L Day, the U.S. attack was launched. Assault boats rushed to the beach, loaded with men expecting fierce resistance. But there was almost none. At the end of the first day, sixty thousand troops were on the beaches. The land shone with peaceful fields and crops and bright wild flowers. The veterans of the bloody battles of Palau, Guadalcanal, and Iwo Jima looked around in amazement. They thought it was an April Fools' joke.

Okinawa is a large island, sixty miles long and, in places, ten miles wide, the most populated of the Ryukyu Islands; a land of small farms cultivating rice, sugar, and sweet potatoes. It's shaped like a barbell, wide at either end, with a two-mile-wide isthmus in the middle, where the landings occurred. Two nearby airfields were quickly overrun. By the end of the second day, units of the First Marine Division had separated the southern third of the island from the northern two thirds. Uncertain where the enemy was, the U.S. commander, Lt. Gen. Simon Bolivar Buckner, sent troops to both ends of the island. It took nearly a week to find the enemy.

The Japanese commander, Lt. Gen. Mitsuru Ushijima, was waiting. He knew the U.S. forces could not be stopped. His only hope was to delay and perhaps thwart an invasion of Japan itself. Abandoning the beaches and open ground as indefensible, he had, instead, dug in on the southern end of the island, where the land flared up into steep fortress-like hills and jagged limestone cliffs, forming a natural, nearly impenetrable wall.

At the foot of these hills, the Japanese had laid mine fields and dug trenches where riflemen armed with grenades and mortars waited. Behind them, in the hills, were machine gun nests and, higher still, heavy artillery. The limestone cliffs were honeycombed with natural caves that the Japanese expanded, using Okinawan laborers, into intricate tunnels and caverns, some large enough to hold an entire company of men. These fortifications stretched across the island, making it difficult and sometimes impossible for tanks and trucks to maneuver. Behind these fortifications were more than 100,000 battle-hardened veterans of the Japanese Thirty-second Army.

General Ushijima's plan was to separate the Americans from their machines, their supporting tanks and armor, and force them into bloody and costly hand-to-hand combat.

Delay the Americans, slow them, chew them up, make them pay a high price for every inch of ground.

By the middle of April, the U.S. forces had reached the southern hills and were on the offensive. Sugar Loaf Hill, Horseshoe and Half Moon Hills, and Conical Hill stood like fortresses. The Americans were out in the open under a constant barrage of machine guns and mortars spewing shrapnel and broken rock. Advances were counted in yards.

Then, in May, the rain started falling steadily. Roads became sticky with mud and jammed with traffic. Tanks and trucks stalled in muddy sinkholes. Soon no man went forward without carrying fuel, ammo, or food, and on the return bringing back the wounded and the dead.

Five weeks after the campaign began, the war that had been going on in Europe for almost six years ended. But there was hardly a moment to celebrate. The Pacific war against the Japanese went on.

It took eighty-three days, nearly three months, before the bloodiest fighting of the Pacific war ended. The U.S. losses: 11,933 men killed, 39,119 wounded, and more than 26,000 other casualties, mostly victims of battle fatigue, too traumatized to go on fighting.

The Japanese losses included 110,000 killed and 10,550 taken prisoner. Rather than surrender, on June 22, the day the campaign officially ended, the Japanese commander, General Ushijima, ordered his own decapitation in a ceremonial suicide. A few days earlier, General Buckner, the American commander, had been struck by a piece of shrapnel from a nearby artillery burst and died within minutes. In all, our Okinawan victory resulted in the deaths of more than 207,000 people, including thousands of civilian Okinawans. These terrible losses led to outcries in the American press. General Douglas MacArthur, who had conducted most of his Pacific campaigns with little loss of life, accused the generals and admirals in charge of the Okinawan campaign of "sacrificing thousands of American soldiers because they insisted on driving the Japanese off the island." Instead, he said, they should have cordoned off the southern end of the island and waited for the Japanese to surrender.

In Japan, the stunning loss of Okinawa left no doubt about the end of the war, and their leaders began to consider the unthinkable—surrender. On August 6, 1945, the atom bomb was dropped on Hiroshima. That single bomb killed 66,000 people and injured 69,000. Ten thousand people were never found. Three days later, another atomic bomb dropped on Nagasaki resulted in the deaths and injury of 64,000 people.

The Japanese surrendered and World War II ended. The official ceremony took place on September 2, 1945, on the battleship *Missouri* in Tokyo Bay, exactly three years, eight months, and one week after the attack on Pearl Harbor.

Literature Circle Questions

Use these questions and the activities that follow to get more out of the experience of reading *Heroes Don't Run* by Harry Mazer.

1. In which ocean would you find Okinawa? What country is less than three hundred miles away from Okinawa?

2. Marines have specific words for many common objects, including boots, guns, and the floor. For at least one of these objects, list the term you would use if you were a Marine. Can you think of any other Marine terms from the story?

3. According to the letter you read in chapter 5, who is Adam hoping to honor by going to the Pacific?

4. Whose permission does Adam need to join the Marines? Why is he in a hurry to sign up?

5. Briefly describe the injuries Adam suffers on Okinawa. Besides these injuries, how is Adam affected by the war, based on what you read in chapter 22?

6. Which people does Adam contact after his return to the United States? If you were returning home after being away in another country, whom would you contact first?

7. Imagine you are Adam's grandfather and Adam has asked you to sign the papers that will allow him to become a Marine. How would you respond to Adam? If you think you would sign the papers, explain why. If you think you would choose to not sign the papers, explain why you would be reluctant to do so.

8. On page 94, Adam quotes his platoon sergeant, Rosie: "Sometimes you had to do things you didn't want to do, but it was right to do them, so you did them." Does this quote apply to your own life? Describe a time when you had to do something you didn't want to do but did it anyway because you felt it was right.

9. Reread Adam's letters to his mother on pages 78 and 90. Describe one way in which these letters misrepresent the truth about Adam's experience. In your own words, why do you think Adam was not entirely honest with his mother?

10. In chapter 25, when Adam is home in Bakersfield, he says about the war, "We made a better world." Who do you think he means by "we"? From

Adam's perspective, how might the world be a better place than it was at the beginning of the story?

11. On page 29, Sergeant Bessie tells the recruits, "What you learn here is going to save your life." Based on what you read about boot camp and about the battle on Okinawa, use details from the text to explain whether you think this statement is true or not true.

12. In the story you just read, Adam makes promises to several other characters, including Grandpa, Helen, and Rosie. Imagine one year has passed since the end of the war. Choose one promise you think Adam is likely to keep and, using your imagination, describe how he might keep it. (Hint: Some of Adam's promises can be found in chapters 18 and 24.)

13. In which skill does Ben score the mark of "expert"? Why does he decline the offer to stay on Parris Island as an instructor? Do you support Ben's decision? What decision would you have made if you were Ben?

14. On page 84, Adam says, "I'm no hero. I'm not brave." Do you believe Adam is a hero? Do you believe he is brave? If yes, explain why. If not, choose another character from the story and explain why you think that person is brave or heroic. Be sure to include specific examples from the story in your answer.

15. With whom does Adam exchange letters in the story? Did you enjoy reading the letters Adam sent and received? Why do you think the author chose to have his characters write letters about their experiences?

Note: These questions are keyed to Bloom's Taxonomy *as follows: Knowledge: 1–3; Comprehension: 4–5; Application: 6–8; Analysis: 9–10; Synthesis: 11–13; Evaluation: 14–15*

Activities

1. In the story you just read, Bea writes Adam a letter in which she uses symbols or pictures in the place of words. For example, instead of writing 'I', Bea draws an eye and instead of writing, 'Bea', she draws a bee. Write a letter to a friend using pictographs similar to these. You can use the letter to say something about the book or just to tell your friend how you are doing.

2. Using colored pencils, crayons, or markers, design an alternate cover for *Heroes Don't Run.* Think carefully about the people and places from the story as you choose who and what to feature on the cover. Remember that a cover should make people want to open the book and read it.

3. Create a map to show Adam's journey back and forth across the United States. Your map should include at least four points: Bakersfield, California; Syracuse, New York; Parris Island, South Carolina; and San Diego, California. If you can

think of anywhere else Adam stopped along the way, you should include that as well. Trace Adam's route and draw symbols showing what he did in each place. Be sure to include a legend to show what each symbol means.

Other Books by This Author:
A Boy No More, Simon & Schuster (September 2004)
A Boy at War: A Novel of Pearl Harbor, Aladdin (November 2002)
The Wild Kid, Aladdin (July 2000)
The Last Mission, Laurel Leaf (February 1981)
Snow Bound, Laurel Leaf (January 1975)

Harry Mazer has been writing books for teenagers for nearly thirty years on a variety of topics, including divorce, war, survival, romance, and family relationships. His *Snow Bound* has become a classic young adult survival story. His autobiographical *The Last Mission* stands among the most popular stories about World War II. And the American Library Association lists *The Solid Gold Kid*, written with his wife, Norma, as one of the 100 Best of the Best Books for Young Adults published between 1967 and 1992.